REALITY CHECK

LARSSON SIBLINGS
BOOK 4

EVIE MITCHELL

THUNDER THIGHS PUBLISHING

Editors: Nicole Wilson, Evermore Editing
http://www.evermoreediting.wixsite.com/info
Illustrator: Laras Putri

ACKNOWLEDGEMENT OF COUNTRY

I acknowledge the Traditional Custodians of the lands on which I write, the Ngunnawal people, and pay my respect to elders both past and present.

I acknowledge the continued and deep spiritual relationship of the Australian Aboriginal and Torres Strait Islander peoples' to this land, and their unique cultural and spiritual relationships to the land, waters and seas and their rich contribution to society.

Always was, always will be.

To my husband.
This book releases on our anniversary and I just
wanted to say thanks.
Thanks for eighteen years of amazing
adventures, beautiful memories, and glorious
love.
Thanks for letting me annoy you every day.
Through bears, beats, and Battlestar Galactica,
I love you.

CONTENT WARNING AND TERMINOLOGY

This book contains graphic and explicit descriptions of sex. The book features a surprise pregnancy, hate-to-love-you, and forced proximity.

While all care has been taken to ensure representation is respectful and inclusive, my sensitivity readers and my personal experience is limited to our own knowledge and understanding. If there is anything in the book that raises concerns for you, please feel free to reach out to EvieMitchellAuthor@gmail.com.

REALITY CHECK

Liv

Unemployed, homeless and pregnant - not how I intended to spend this Thanksgiving.

To be fair, I quit my job, and no one could have predicted the flood in my apartment.

The baby? Well, that's on me.

A tipsy hook-up at my brother's wedding, a failed condom, and suddenly I'm stuck with my nemesis, Ian Campbell.

The man is infuriating - he looks like a red-haired Big Foot, is built like a lumberjack, and acts like a refined laird of some crumbling castle.

He's confusing, irritating and... kissable?

No, no way. There is absolutely no possible universe in which I'm falling for the Sasquatch... right?

Ian

Liv 'The Harpy' Larsson is pregnant is my baby. How the good God did that happen?

I mean, I know how it happened. Those memories don't seem to want to quit.

But now she's in my house. And my car. And at my work. And we're going to pregnancy classes and buying diapers, and she's suddenly not so much a harpy as happy.

Wait. No. Do I like Liv?

Is this... love?

Warning: This book is inspired by reality TV, strong scotch, and lumberjacks. So, get thee a man, a camera, and settle in — this read will have you questioning if hate is really such a bad thing.

PROLOGUE

Liv

August 15

"And so," I said, holding up my glass and tilting it toward the happy couple. "In summary, welcome to the family, Ella. Sorry, you got stuck with my useless lump of a brother. But at least you get me."

Laughter exploded around the tent while Gunnar, the groom in question, rolled his eyes, subtly flipping me the bird.

"To Ella and Gunnar!" I declared, ignoring my brother's antics.

"To Ella and Gunnar!" The room toasted,

glasses clinking, laughter, and conversation swelling.

I sat down, lifting my glass to take a sip of the sparkling wine, heart aching with gladness, hope, love, and a little envy that my brother had finally found his one.

My younger sister, Astrid, leaned over, laughter on her lips. "Great speech."

"Thanks. I thought you'd enjoy the roasting."

The wedding ceremony had taken place in Gunnar and Ella's yard, the altar positioned out to face the ocean. It had been beautiful, sentimental, and above all, them. My brother and his beautiful bride pledging to love one another forever under a clear blue sky.

The reception had kicked off immediately. A large tent covered in garlands and fairy lights provided some protection from the afternoon sun. Now that darkness had fallen, the long picnic tables that were covered in white fabric and pretty lights created a magical backdrop for this perfect night.

The caterers were food vans, and guests were invited to help themselves. There were no assigned tables, no formal placemats, just good food, great music, and lots of laughs.

"Great wedding." A plate of food landed beside me with a thump, the accompanying body settling onto the bench seat taking up any available space.

"Really?" I asked, raising an eyebrow at the intruder as he squirmed his way in, his thigh pressing against mine. "You couldn't have found another table? *Any* other table?"

Ian Campbell grinned at me, his teeth flashing through the red hair of his unkempt beard. "Look around, love. There's not a space to be had."

I glanced about, seeing the truth of his words. With gritted teeth, I turned away, reaching for my wine glass.

He lifted a slider, managing not to drop a bite in his crazy beard.

"How's the junk TV going?" he asked a moment later, spearing a forkful of potato salad.

I arched an eyebrow. "Excuse me?"

Since when do you care?

"Ye're still doing those reality TV shows, yeah?"

I crossed my arms, bristling. "I didn't realize we were small-talk kind of people."

"Settle down, Harpy." He lifted his beer, taking a sip. "I'm just being polite."

"Don't. It doesn't look good on you."

He chuckled, turning to give me his full attention.

"Are you saying something else does?"

"Yes." I pushed to a stand, giving him my chilliest smile, the one I saved for misogynists, criminals, and people who didn't like puppies. And Ian. "Death looks great on you."

I turned on my heel, walking away as Ian's laughter followed me.

I made it to the dance floor just as the singer cleared his throat, drawing attention to the small stage.

"And now, the first dance. If the bride and groom will take the floor?"

I watched my brother lead his bride to the dance floor, blinking back tears as they began to sway to a cover of Unconditional by Freya Ridings.

"They're gorgeous," Astrid whispered beside me, wiping tears from her cheek.

"Yeah, they are." I leaned into her, wrapping my arms around her middle. "They're perfect."

As the song wound up, we all clapped, laughing as Gunnar tipped Ella back in a graceful dip before pulling her back into his arms for a kiss.

We cheered and catcalled, Ian raising two fingers to his mouth to let out an earsplitting wolf whistle.

With a smile a mile wide, Ella swept her

arm out, inviting us to join them on the dance floor.

I looked around, catching sight of my father leading my mother onto the cleared space. My heart gave a little flop as he pulled mom close, holding her tight.

Oh, to have a love like theirs.

Forty years on they still looked at each other with hearts in their eyes.

The singer started back up, doing a slowed down less country and more soulful rock cover of Kane Brown's Thunder in the Rain.

"Come on." My brother, Erik, lifted Laura's hand, pressing a kiss to his fiancé's knuckles. "Let's dance."

On his other side, Gabby, my youngest sibling fiancé, led him onto the dance floor, cajoling Rune with a shimmy of her shoulders, setting her breasts jiggling. With a sigh and a roll of his eyes, he pulled her into his arms, bending to kiss her.

Astrid leaned closer, sighing. "It sucks to be the single ones."

"Preach."

"I wanna dance too."

"Come on then," I told her, linking our fingers. "Let's dance."

Stepping out with a laugh, we slung arms

around each other, swaying together in time to the music.

"This playlist is very country!" Astrid called as the singer transitioned into Sam Hunt's Body Like A Back Road.

I nodded, laughing as Rune allowed Gabby to grind up against him, his body moving from side to side in what I could only call an awkward white guy shuffle. Beside him, the local Sheriff and his wife, Honey, ground together, their bodies pure magic as they performed a kind of flamenco-cross-country swing.

"Come on." A hand caught mine, skilfully spinning me away from Astrid and into the thick chest of a giant. "Let's give the good Sheriff a run for his money."

I'd later blame this moment on shock – really, it was the only reasonable explanation for what happened next.

Ian and I danced. We moved around the dance floor in tandem, our bodies coming together in a way that felt intimate and sensual. We were in sync, perfectly so.

I hated it even as I loved it. The two emotions coalescing into a frustrating burn.

The world fell away as he guided me around the dancefloor, his body pressed to mine.

"Just because you can dance doesn't mean I like you," I told him as Ian twirled me out and pulled me back in.

"You know I'd never presume that ye'd find me even the least bit palatable." He grinned, twisting me this way and then that, his hands warm and confident on my hips. "Even I'm not that stupid."

And therein lay the problem. Ian Campbell wasn't stupid. Not even a fraction. Not even close. The man completed degrees in his spare time, for goodness sake. And he did them for fun. Fun!

"Ye ready, lass?"

I blinked. "For?"

"The finale."

He dipped me, catching my neck and guiding me low. Around us, the crowd erupted, clapping and cheering as he gently lifted me back up, my body sliding along his.

"I hate you," I whispered, glaring at him even as my body gave a little shiver.

His eyes flashed with amusement and something darker. "The feeling, I can assure ye, is entirely mutual."

With a fake laugh, I tossed my hair, stepping back from him, clapping and joining in the festivities, throwing off the faint kick of attraction that had begun burning in my belly.

No way in hell am I attracted to Ian Campbell.

"Here." Astrid handed me a glass of water, grinning as she watched me suck it down.

"What?"

She gave a half-shoulder shrug. "Nothing."

I glared over my glass. "Bullshit."

She laughed, turning away. "You know what they say, hate and love are two sides of the same coin."

I rolled my eyes, watching as Ian claimed another partner, doing with her what he'd done with me.

Only, it really has to be said, far less impressively.

I shoved that thought aside, pressing the cool glass to my warm forehead.

It's just the wedding vibes getting to you. You're tougher than this Liv.

Feeling suddenly over warm, I moved through the crowd seeking the cool night air. Outside the tent, I blended into the shadows, following the twinkling fairy lights that led down a short walk onto Ella and Gunnar's private beach.

With a sigh, I made my way to the old wooden boathouse, laughing when I found the inside similarly lit with lights and some bedding.

"Oh, Ella." I shook my head, knowing this had to be the work of my sister-in-law. It wouldn't surprise me to learn that she'd set this up, likely expecting that there would be at least one wedding guest who'd need to crash the night after consuming too much alcohol.

"Liv?"

I turned, finding Ian coming down the beach, his shoes in one hand and a bottle of wine in the other.

I sighed, plucking one of the blankets from the bed and wrapping it around my shoulders as I walked to meet him, the sand cool beneath my feet.

"Couldn't leave me alone for five minutes?"

His lips quirked, one bushy eyebrow cocking. "I'd say it's the other way around, lass. You've found my bed."

I paused, suddenly registering the masculine scent coming from the blanket around my shoulders.

"Oh."

He grinned, gesturing towards the small dock. "Come sit with me?"

I'd never be quite sure why I followed him. Maybe because he asked rather than told. Maybe because I felt a little melancholy. Either way you looked at it, I ended up sitting beside Ian, sharing his wine.

"You ever feel lost?" I asked, finding myself suddenly morose as we stared at the moonlight shimmering on the waves.

I felt rather than saw Ian turn, considering me in the dim light. "Depends."

"On?"

"If I want to be lost or not."

I laughed, glancing at him. "You want to be lost?"

"Sure. The best adventures start when the trail ends."

"Are you a hallmark card?"

He grinned, sipping from the wine bottle.

I processed his words, turning them over in my mind.

"You know, sometimes you can be a decent human being."

"Sometimes?" He bumped me with his arm. "Hardly a recommendation."

"Aye," I said, trying to imitate his accent. "And ye'll do well not to push yer luck."

He laughed, lifting the wine to his lips and looking back out at the ocean. "Do ye want a family, Liv?"

I shrugged. "I haven't really thought about it."

Liar, liar, pants on fire.

"Why not? A pretty lass like you should be beating the men away."

I reached for the bottle, plucking it from his hands and sucking down a sip. "I've got a goal. I've worked hard to get where I am."

"As queen of reality shows?"

I frowned. "Is that judgment I hear?"

He shrugged, taking back the bottle. "Always thought you were better than that."

I bristled, part of me angry at his judgment, another annoyed that he echoed my own thoughts. "We all start somewhere. My plan isn't to be in reality forever. Well, not the entertainment reality anyway."

"No?"

"Mm. I wanna move into film. Movies and documentaries. I want to show life in all its strange forms."

"Really?"

It was my turn to bump him. "Don't sound so surprised."

He caught my chin, turning me to face him, his gaze searching mine. "I'm not surprised, Liv. I'm pleased for ye. It's been a long time since you sounded so excited."

I swallowed, pulling away from him and turning to look back out at the water, attempting to hide how much I wanted this.

"Yeah... well... it's gotta happen first. I should know in the next few months once they go through all the interviews and whatnot."

"And I have no doubt you'll make it so. If nothing else ye're persistent."

I laughed, moving to shove him, but he shifted, catching my hand and pulling me into him.

"W-w-what are you doing?" I asked as he bent his head.

"Kissing ye."

With that declaration, he closed the gap between us, pressing a hot, rough, demanding kiss to my mouth. His tongue took advantage of my surprise, slipping between my lips and stroking mine with delicious intention.

For a moment, I remained stiff, shock holding me rigid against him. Then he made a noise, a mix between a groan and a grunt, and I melted, kissing him back.

Oh, God. Why am I enjoying this? This is Ian. Ian! You hate Ian! Stop, Liv! Abort! Abort!

But it appeared I didn't need to like him to want to sleep with him.

"Fuck," he muttered, pulling back slightly to trail kisses down my neck. "Ye taste like the devil."

I huffed out a laugh, his beard rasping against my skin in a way I'd never have thought I'd find arousing. "You're one to talk."

He bit the seam of my shoulder,

immediately licking away the sting. "Shall we do this, lass? Or am I to leave you now?"

I glanced back at the boathouse and the cozy bed inside. "We can never tell another soul. One and done."

"Of course." He grinned. "No one'd believe us anyway. Ye hate my guts too much."

He stood, helping me up, pulling me into his arms and kissing me again.

"Gonna fuck you into next week," he muttered against my lips. "Gotta get this outta our systems."

A deep ache began to pulse between my thighs, my body tightening at his words. "Then you better get this over with."

He boosted me up, my arms and legs automatically wrapping around him, holding on as he walked us to the tiny cabin, his rigid cock a teasing heat between my legs.

I'd blame it on the wine. Or the ocean setting. Or perhaps the romance of a perfect wedding. I'd blame the next hour on anything but what it was – pure animal attraction.

In a fumble, we stripped each other, lips tasting newly revealed skin. I expected missionary Ian pounding over me and perhaps a small tingle of an orgasm if I were lucky.

I got an explosion.

He pushed me down, flipped me over,

pulled my arms forward, and covered my back with his front.

"Gonna fuck ye dirty," he whispered against the shell of my ear. "Yell if it gets too much."

With that, he pulled back, one hand still holding mine in front of me, his other rolling on a condom.

"I don't have all night," I complained, my wet arousal coating my thighs.

Instead of answering, he slapped a palm against my butt, immediately cupping the area and rubbing the sting away. His teeth grazed my shoulder, nipping at the sensitive skin.

"For once in ye life, shut your mouth and let me fucking work."

I opened my mouth again, a retort on the tip of my tongue, but Ian beat me to the punch, sliding his cock into me, thrusting hard and fast, violently seating himself, possessing my body.

"Fuck!" I gasped, throwing my head back, my body clenching and clutching at his intrusion. "Fuck!"

"Good?" He asked, a dark chuckle on his lips.

"Shut up and keep moving."

He answered my demand with another spank, my pussy clenching around his long member.

"Ah, I see you like a little pain with ye pleasure."

He let go of my hands, lifting me up.

"What are you—" I broke off, my body bucking as sensations ratcheted through me, each building rapidly. He pulled my nipples, pinching my areolas with just the right amount of pain to send me spiralling.

"Ian!"

His body began to move, his cock thrusting in and out of me, hitting all the deliciously sensitive nerve endings.

Oh, God, how is this so good!?

Ian pulled back slightly, moving a little, changing his angle. My eyes rolled back into my head; a strangled moan ripped from my throat.

Holy God of Thunder!

He answered me with a grunt, picking up his pace, his body rough and heavy, the weight and heat of him adding to the moment.

I felt like a peasant girl being ravaged by a conquering laird. My pleasure secondary to his release.

The thought tipped me over, my body spasming as wave after wave of hot, heated bliss crashed over me, every nerve in my body filled with liquid heat.

"Ian!"

"Fuck!"

He slapped my ass, sending me into another pleasurable spin.

"Fuck you," I grunted, pushing myself back against his cock. "Stop spanking me."

"Stop enjoying it."

Ian abandoned my nipples, one hand fisting in my hair, the other sliding down my body to find my clit.

"Ye're gonna come again, Liv. And this time, I'm coming too."

He pulled my head back, tipping my face until he could suck on my neck. His fingers circled, teasing then stroking even as his cock ground into me, the rough friction turning me into a whimpering mess.

As promised, I came in a wet, messy moment of utter perfection. Biting the inside of my cheek to keep from screaming, I arched back, offering myself to him in filthy submission.

Fuck you, Ian Campbell.

I hated him. I loathed his power over my body. I hated every minute of this.

So good. So goddamned good. Again, again, again!

I slipped forward, my body crushed by his as he came, dropping us both into the bed.

We lay for a moment, gasping for breath,

his weight pressing me into the mattress, reality intruding.

Ah, reality check, Liv. You just fucked Ian. Ian, who you hate. Ian, who hates you. Ian fucking Campbell.

Shit.

He rolled off, giving my ass a little spank.

"Be right back. Gotta take care of the condom."

He walked to the bathroom, closing the door.

I lay like a stunned mullet, still and silent, shocked by the pleasure still bouncing through my body and the stark reality that I'd just had sex with Ian.

Well, shit.

I scrambled up, tossing my dress over my head and grabbing a blanket to wrap around myself and hide my braless state. In a mad dash, I found my shoes but couldn't locate my underwear – bra or panties.

I heard Ian flush the toilet, the faucet turning on as he washed his hands.

Go, go, go!

I left, heading back up to the party, finding the majority of wedding guests were still dancing the night away.

Acting as if I hadn't just had the most mind-blowing sexual experience of my life.

I left the party, heading inside Gunnar's house to clean and find some underwear. I met Astrid at the door.

"Hey, you okay? You disappeared."

"Mm, fine. Just needed to cool down."

Astrid laughed, slapping my shoulder. "You really burned up that dancefloor. Pity you hate Ian so much. You guys looked amazing together."

With a gulp, I nodded, baring my teeth in what I hoped was a sarcastic grin. "Yeah, such a pity."

I cleaned up and then returned to the party, finding myself spinning around the dance floor with my father.

"One day, this will be you, Livvy," he said, gesturing around the tent. "You and some dashing young man set to carry you away."

My gaze caught on the far side of the tent, Ian's red hair sticking out amongst the blonde, black, and brunette.

He stood leaning against a table, arms crossed, a small smile on his lips, his hair wild, beard crazy, his jacket discarded, leaving him in black suit pants and a white collared shirt with the sleeves rolled up to his biceps.

Why is that so attractive?

Our gaze met, caught, held.

As Dad continued to get sentimental, I

watched Ian, some foreign feeling taking up residence in my chest.

Finally, the song finished, and Dad let go of me to clap with the rest of the crowd. I did the same on autopilot, unable to break Ian's stare.

He inclined his head towards the entrance, one eyebrow arching in question. It was a blatant invitation, a request to join him once again.

With deliberation, I turned my back on him, drawing the last of my shredded dignity around me, putting space between us.

Back in your box, Ian. Back to the other side of the picket line.

"Another?" I asked my dad, lifting my arms in question.

"Always for my second favorite daughter."

With a laugh, I let him take the lead, whirling me around the dance floor, grinning at all his jokes.

When I next looked back, Ian was gone.

CHAPTER 1

Liv

November 17

I sucked desperately on the ginger candy, willing the nausea that had plagued me for the last month to disappear. I didn't have time for whatever illness currently plagued me. I had a doctor's appointment this afternoon, but in the meantime, I had a job offer to accept.

Thinking about this new opportunity sent my stomach into another spiral.

It's only the most important meeting of your life. Calm down.

I drew in a long breath, pressing the remains of the candy to the roof of my mouth, trying to suck at whatever tiny bit of ginger remained.

You can do this. You got this, you glorious, badass boss of a woman.

I checked my watch, noting it was ten minutes to the meeting.

Always be early.

I kicked off my flats, swapping them for heels. I shimmied a little, straightening the skirt of my corporate but fashionable navy dress.

You got this, Liv. Go crush it.

I exited my office, giving a nod to James, my assistant. "I'm just heading over to Bob's office. Do you need anything?"

"Nope, but good luck!" He flashed thumbs-up at me. "Not that you need it."

With a sly grin, I nodded, setting off through the office, heading for the elevator that would take me up to the C-suite.

I'd worked at Catch 22 Productions for over a decade now, clawing myself up the ranks, chipping away at the glass ceilings, and carving out a niche in this male-dominated company. I'd started as a high school intern, moving across the country to work summers in LA. Once I'd graduated, I'd studied at the American Film Institute, working at Catch 22 every evening and weekend, then graduated and took on any job I could in an effort to cement my place in the company.

It'd worked. Five years ago, I'd been asked to build the reality TV branch of the company. I'm sure they expected a knock-off Real House Wives, or perhaps an equivalent of Keeping up with the Kardashians. Instead, I'd built us a brand of reality shows with heart. The shows we produced had integrity, honesty, and I'd built that arm into one of our most successful products.

Shows like The Queen of Clean, where we helped people turn their lives around through organization and education. Or Home Bound, where we worked with a celebrity and Habitat for Humanity to build homes for people who would otherwise never have the opportunity to own their own house. Or Country Crush, a dating show where we took eligible singles out to lonely farms across America, all in hopes of them finding their one true love.

Proudly, Country Crush had resulted in three babies, eight marriages, and one town mayor writing to thank me for raising awareness of his town. Their tourism had doubled thanks to our show – allowing them to reopen some of the dying businesses and giving locals a much-needed economic boost.

But I wanted a new challenge. I wanted

documentaries. I wanted to have an opportunity to go to the next level and produce series and shows that made people question what they knew. I wanted to sink my teeth into topics and explore. I'd pushed the boundaries with all of my shows, exploring issues like race, sexuality, gender, disability, and class in digestible but gentle ways. Documentaries would be an opportunity to push the envelope to explore the meaty issues.

The elevator binged softly, the doors sliding open to the C-Suite. With a bracing breath, I stepped into the push suite, grinning at Jenny, Bob's executive assistant.

"He's just finishing up with Robbie Huynh," Jenny said with a grin. "He's such a nice boy." She lifted a hand fanning herself. "And ooh! Those arms? If I were twenty years younger...."

I grinned, giving her a wink. "I don't know, Jenny. I hear Aussies don't mind an older woman. Look at Hugh Jackman and Deborra-Lee Furness, there's like twelve years between them."

Jenny waved me off. "Oh, go on with you. That boy has more models and movie stars throwing themselves at him than a tomcat on a Saturday night."

I couldn't help but laugh at the analogy. Jenny was famous for strange examples.

"I thought Robbie was still in Australia?"

She shrugged. "Says he's got a proposal for Bob. Though goodness knows it's probably not going to be what he wants. Bob's set to keep him as the next big heartthrob. Wants to farm him out to some superhero movies. I think Robbie wants to explore his artistic side."

I nodded, glancing at the door.

"Anyway, take a seat. Bob shouldn't be long. Can I get you something?"

I shook my head. "Nope, all good, thanks."

I settled on one of the comfortable chairs in his waiting area, listening to the rhythmic clicking of Jenny's keyboard while mentally going over my notes. My numbers were excellent, and my ideas sound. In five years, I'd only needed to cancel two programs after the pilots had flopped. Both, I would point out, were ideas I'd inherited.

You've got this, Liv. There's no way he's saying no.

The door to Bob's office opened, Robbie stepping out.

"Thanks again," he said, shaking Bob's hand.

"I'll call you Thursday to discuss further."

Bob clapped a hand on Robbie's shoulder. "And don't worry, kid. We'll find the right fit for you."

"Yeah, thanks." Robbie turned away but not before I saw his jaw clench.

Bob watched him leave the suite, shaking his head before turning to me. "Liv, come on in."

"Good meeting?" I asked, following him into the room and closing the door behind us.

"You know how it is." He waved a hand around the room, settling behind his giant wooden desk. "These kids come to Hollywood expecting to win an Oscar with some arty-farty indie shit. Sometimes you gotta be cruel to be kind. He'll come round."

I nodded, biting my tongue to keep from reminding Bob that Robbie's contract with us was up in March.

"Now, let's talk about you." He leaned back in his chair, knitting his hands over his solid belly. "You applied for the films job. Why?"

Excitement sizzled up my veins, those butterflies taking flight in my belly once more. I tried to ignore the accompanying nausea, swallowing hard.

"Well, Bob, let's be honest. Films have floundered in the last three years— documentaries, in particular, is a black pit of despair. We both know Jim wasn't engaged in the lead-up to his retirement. We need fresh blood. Edgy content. New life. In the interview I gave to the panel last month, I outlined—"

He stopped me with a dismissive wave of his hand. "This ain't an interview, Liv. I've already made a decision. I'm just wondering why you wanted to leave your position. You ain't docos, you're entertainment. And you're good at it."

I blinked, processing his words. "I'm sorry?"

"Your place is in entertainment, Hun. I'm sorry, but I'm giving the job to Malone."

"Malone?" I repeated, shock rendering me incapable of further cognition.

"Yeah. The boy worked through documentaries in his undergrad."

I cleared my throat, feeling my chances at this job slipping away. "But Bob, I worked for two years in documentaries and film. I put in the hours through college. And shifting me from reality makes more sense than moving him from—"

"My mind is made up."

"Bob. I heard the desperation creeping into my tone. "I need this. My numbers are solid. My team are trained. Please. There's no reason for me to stay."

"Actually, those numbers are the exact

reason we want you to stay." He leaned forward, his rotund belly pressing against his desk. "Your productions are one of our biggest earners. We can't afford to lose that."

I floundered for a moment, my mouth opening and closing, but no noise came out. I forcefully brought myself under control, yanking back my emotions and stuffing them into a little box.

"So, what you're saying is that I'm too successful for you to lose?" I finally asked.

"Them the facts, Liv."

"And the board agreed to this?"

He nodded.

"And the selection panel?"

He sighed, running a hand over his face. "Look, you were always a shoo-in for it. But like I said, we can't afford to lose you."

I nodded, an eerie calm settling over me. "How long?"

"How long what?" he asked, a frown marring his forehead.

"How long do I stay in reality? How long before you let me move elsewhere?"

He shrugged. "I don't know. How long is a piece of string?"

I nodded. "And there's no option for Malone and me to share the film role?"

He laughed. "No, definitely not. That wouldn't be fair to the kid."

I nodded again. "What about allowing me to produce a few documentaries and film features a year? Maybe one a quarter?"

"Liv, please. I need you to focus on reality. We both know that's where your talent lies."

I sucked in a breath, taking that gut punch.

"Okay, so just to clarify. I was the successful candidate for the position, but you and the board decided to give it to Malone because I'm too successful in my job. And you cannot foresee any possible scenario where I could produce features at this time. Is that right?"

He nodded, grinning. "Yeah, that about sums it up."

I stood, smoothing down my skirt before holding a hand out for him to shake. He took it automatically, the smile on his lips turning into a frown.

"Bob, thank you. It's been an absolute privilege working for Catch-22. As per my contract, consider this my two weeks' notice. I'm meant to be on vacation as of tomorrow, so I'll have my desk cleared out by lunch today." I dropped his hand, stepping back. "I'm happy to do a handover with my replacement once they start. My suggestion would be to look at

Caroline. She's got both the experience and creativity. But considering this company seems to still be a boy's club, if you don't want Caroline, look at Omar. He's young but knows people. He'll do right by you."

I paused, considering if there was anything else I needed to say.

Nope. You're good.

With a final nod, I turned on my heel, reaching for the door. "Goodbye, Bob."

That galvanized my former boss into action. "Liv! Wait!"

I ripped the door open, striding through the suite.

"See ya later, Hun!" Jenny called from her desk.

"Bye Jenny. And FYI, I just quit." Saying it aloud freed something in me, a weight lifting from my shoulders. "If you wanna catch up for coffee, let me know."

I stepped into the waiting elevator, hitting my floor. As the doors began to slide close, Bob exited his office shouting my name while Jenny stared at me, her mouth open, eyes wide.

Back on my floor, I headed immediately for my office, beginning to throw all my personal items into a box.

"Um... Liv?"

I glanced up, finding James loitering at the door. "Come in, you can help me pack."

He entered, glancing at the box and then at me. "Um, what's happening?"

"Oh, I quit. They refused to give me the job, so I just... quit." I shrugged.

"What will you do?" He asked, opening up one of my drawers and beginning to automatically sort through the items.

"I don't know yet." I paused, tipping my head to the side as I considered my options. "Actually, I know exactly what I'm gonna do."

"Yeah?"

"Mmhm, start my own company."

James coughed, eyes wide, eyebrows lifted. "Seriously?"

"Uh-huh." I finished stuffing my things into the box and then gestured at the awards hung around the room. "Can you hold these for me? I'll send someone to pick them and anything else up later this afternoon."

"Of course." He glanced around. "Is there anything else you need?"

I thought for a minute. "Send me my personal contact list, not the one the company keeps on file. That's it."

I lifted the heavy box and then paused. "James, if you want in on this, let me know. I'd love to have you once I get this process started."

He swallowed audibly. "Liv, you're the best boss I've ever had. But the pay...."

I laughed, nodding. "I'll call you once it's all sorted. No harm, no foul if it ends up not being for you."

With that, I shifted, placing the box on my hip, grabbed my tote then walked out. I could feel the glances and questions from the bullpen, but I ignored them, secure in my decision.

You're too badass for this place.

Outside, I flagged a cab, settling into the back seat with a sigh.

"Bad day?" the cabby asked with a pointed look at my box of belongings.

"Nope, perfect day."

He took off from the sidewalk, leaving the headquarters of Catch-22 in the rear vision mirror.

My stomach, which had been playing ball up to this moment, rolled, moisture flooding my mouth.

"Pull over!"

I threw the door open, leaning out to vomit in the gutter, my body heaving as I emptied what little I'd consumed today into the street.

"Sorry," I whispered, pulling a tissue from my tote and wiping my mouth. "I think I've picked up a bug. Can't seem to shake it."

"Sure you aren't pregnant?" the cabby asked with a grin. "Seems to be going around at the moment."

I froze, my heart racing as my mind went blank.

Oh shit. Ohhhhhh shit!

The symptoms checked out. The timing might be right too.

"Umm, can you stop by a pharmacy?"

The cabby glanced my way, one eyebrow cocked. "Sure."

Fuck.

CHAPTER 2

Liv

I stared at my landlord, my box of belongings in one arm, my tote holding the dreaded pregnancy test in the other.

"I'm sorry, did you say flooded?"

Warren nodded, grimacing. "Those fucking builders hit a water pipe. Sorry, doll, but your apartment and everyone else on your level are flooded. Whole buildings gotta be evacuated until they can repair the damage. Electric is shot. Ain't safe to do much more than get some valuables and hightail it outta here."

I blinked, processing this news. "Are you saying I have to find a hotel?"

"More like a short-stay apartment. Gonna be weeks if not months before we can fix the damage. Mother fuckers," he swore, shaking his head.

Months!?

"Um, right." I stared at Mrs. Gelder, the old woman had her soaking wet Pekinese-cross tucked under one arm and was struggling to pull a roller suitcase behind her with the other. As I watched, her son arrived, lifting the bag easily and walking her to his car.

"I better go see what I can salvage."

In my apartment, I stared in stunned dismay at the damage. Brown, smelly water squished underfoot and dripped like rain from the ceiling. Every item of clothing, furniture, or knickknack lay in soaked ruin. There was little to recover here.

"Well... fuck."

I shrugged off my jacket, using it to wipe water from my counter and place my box on the semi-dry spot.

"Okay, Liv, you've lived through worse than this moment. Let's prioritize, organize, and mobilize."

My stomach rumbled, reminding me that it'd been a while since I'd managed to keep anything down.

"And then food."

I pulled suitcases from my closet, lining them with garbage bags to keep the water from soaking into the dry inner fabric. I wrung out my saturated clothing before tossing them into the bags and piling them into the suitcases. My paintings were ruined, my photos completely destroyed. Any electrical items would need to be tossed, but I had everything backed up on the cloud so I wasn't worried.

In a surprisingly short amount of time, I'd packed up my life, searching the apartment for any small sentimental item I'd missed. There were none. This apartment in which I'd spent the last three years of my life was surprisingly devoid of personality.

Maybe this is for the best.

The thought popped into my head as I loaded myself into another cab, this time heading for a hotel near the airport.

You can start fresh, try out a new life. A new Liv, if you will.

In the hotel, I handed over my soggy clothing to the concierge, who assured me they'd put a rush on it. In my room, I called the airline to get my flight swapped to the first one out tomorrow and cancel my return. I ordered room service, showered then, wrapped in a cozy robe, I stared at the pregnancy test, my bladder protesting its fullness.

"Okay, Liv. Let's do this."

I read the instructions twice just to ensure I understood completely.

It's just peeing on a stick. Who knew there was an art to this?

Mid-stream I stuck the stick in my pee, grimacing as some splashed on my hand.

I can't believe some women choose to do this.

Fully peed, I lay the stick on the bathroom sink and hit the timer on my phone pacing as I determinedly ignored the test until the alarm went off.

Beep beep beep.

I sucked in a breath and then flipped it over, my heart stuttering to a stop.

Two lines. Positive. I'm pregnant. I'm motherfucking pregnant.

"Oh shit." I dropped onto the toilet, cradling my head in my hands. "Homeless, jobless, pregnant. What am I gonna do now?"

Reality hit, horror dawning.

"Oh, God," I placed a shaky hand on my belly, staring down at my hand. "I'm pregnant with a Sasquatch."

CHAPTER 3

Ian

I poured coffee into my mug, struggling against the haze of exhaustion that had settled on my shoulders.

It was still early enough that none of the guys had arrived at the Thor's Shipbuilding workshop for work yet, but late enough that the first blush of dawn had begun to light the sky.

I watched the sky lighten out the kitchenette window, sipping my coffee and thinking about nothing in particular.

I'd moved into the tiny apartment above the workshop last week. My rental had sold last month, and I'd decided to take the plunge and buy a property. Unfortunately, it wouldn't close until Monday, which left me temporarily homeless. Thankfully, Erik had offered me the loft apartment, and I'd happily accepted.

The tiny apartment had everything I needed – a bed, a small lounge area, and a kitchenette with a breakfast bar. When Erik had adopted his twin boys, he'd moved out of the apartment, leaving it vacant. His sister, Astrid, occasionally stayed here over the college breaks, but the place remained empty for most of the year, only occasionally serving as temporary accommodation for one of our staff.

I lifted the mug to my lips again, the sip getting caught in my throat as I caught sight of a woman wrangling with the lock on our front gate.

Or should I say *the* woman.

Coughing, I dropped the mug in the sink, a curse forming on my tongue as I headed for the stairs.

What the fuck is she doing here?

I didn't pull on boots, instead slipping my socked feet into flip-flops before thundering down the stairs and out into the yard.

The Harpy had managed to get the gate open, her curses audible from across the yard as she struggled to pull a giant suitcase through the small gap she'd left herself.

"What are you doing?"

She froze, her body stiffening as her head twisted slowly in my direction.

"Oh no." She dropped the suitcase, turning fully to me, her hands coming up as if to ward me off. "No, no, no, no, no!"

"Oh, hush ye mouth," I barked, stopping just out of arm's reach from her. I'd learned my lesson, never be within slapping distance of Liv Larsson.

Except when you kiss her...

I shoved the thought away, crossing my arms over my chest, suddenly aware of the fact I wore only socks with flip-flops and a pair of navy boxer shorts.

"What are ye doing here, Liv?" I asked, brazening this out.

She crossed her arms, mimicking my stance. "I think the better question is what are *you* doing here and dressed like—" she waved her hand at me, "—that."

"Staying in the apartment. Not that it's any of ye business."

She blanched her face paling. "Y-y-you're staying here?"

I frowned, suddenly uneasy. "Yeah. Ye got a problem with that?"

She dropped her arms, her hands fluttering for a moment before settling on her belly, covering it in a pose that was all too familiar.

"Ah fuck." I shook my head. "You're pregnant."

Her eyes widened, her face paling further as she stared at me. "How... how did you...?"

I nodded at the possessive hands over her belly. "My sisters have had a parcel of kids between them. Ye think I don't recognize that pose?"

Her gaze dropped, staring for a beat at her hands as if they were foreign objects. She moved, both hands coming up to press against her cheeks.

"I'm gonna be sick."

I stepped back as she bent, her body heaving as she vomited onto the gravel lot.

"Well, shit. Can hardly be mad at you now." I moved, laying hands on her back and gently rubbing. "It'll be alright, lass. Let it up."

I continued to rub her back in what I hoped was a soothing pattern as anger het my blood.

Where's the father? Bet it's some fancy Hollywood type with more money than sense whose abandoned her. I better call the Larsson's and tell them to sharpen the pitchforks.

Liv interrupted my silent tirade, spitting on the ground and then groaning as she straightened, my hands catching her as she stumbled backwards.

"Thanks," she whispered, turning back to

her piled luggage. "Let me just get some water, and I'll go."

"Over my dead body," I told her, reaching for the giant suitcase. "I may not be the most chivalrous male on the planet, but I can at least offer ye a cup of tea while you wait for your family to arrive."

"I can't have—"

"Ginger tea," I interrupted, cutting off her protest. "Come on. I'll bring ye things in."

She stood, wringing her hands together as I easily lifted her luggage, leading the way across the yard.

Even pale and sweaty with greasy hair and vomit breath, Liv took my breath away. Beautiful didn't cut it. She'd always glowed, burning brighter than the rest of us. A lesser man may try to dim that light, but I'd always found it her most attractive trait.

Pity it came attached to that mouth of hers.

Is it, though? You liked that mouth on your—

I killed that thought, mentally imposing Liv vomiting over it.

Pregnant. Needing help. Keep it in your pants, Campbell.

Upstairs I discarded her luggage, then set about making tea. Liv stood awkwardly, her big coat wrapped tight around her as if it were a shield protecting her from me.

"Take a seat before someone thinks ye're a coat rack." I gestured at the barstools, frowning when she didn't respond with a quick retort.

This isn't good.

The kettle boiled, and I poured the water, watching as Liv slid onto one of the stools, slowly dragging her coat off and laying it across her lap. She slumped on her seat, staring at her hands as they rested on the kitchen counter.

"Here." I placed the mug before her, the steam billowing out and sending the strong scent of ginger into the air. "Now, hit me with it. Tell Uncle Ian what's wrong."

Alarm bells rang in my ears when she didn't take the bait, just reached out a hand to pull the mug to her, then wrapped both palms around the warm ceramic.

I waited, expecting Liv to speak. When she remained silent, those alarm bells turned into emergency warnings, loud and insistent.

I yanked the fridge open, removing two bottles of beer. Uncapping them both, I slid one across the counter to her, nodding at it.

"You can't drink it, and I've to be at work in an hour. So, I'll allow ye to sniff it while you tell me what's on yer mind."

She chuckled, the corners of her generous

mouth lifting a few beats before dropping once more.

"I didn't get the film role. I wanted it, Ian. Badly."

That's what this is about? Not the babe?

"There'll be other roles."

"No." She shook her head. "Or at least not at Catch-22. Bob, my boss, made that clear. I'm too valuable doing infotainment. Reality TV pays, and they need me to keep it profitable." She pulled the beer to her face, inhaling deeply.

"I quit my job."

I sucked in a breath. "But you love working there."

She shrugged. "I thought I did. But now, looking back, I realize I had to fight for everything. Every idea, every new production, every budget." She looked up, pinning me with her baby blues. "They used to do business meetings at the local men's club. I'd have to get a readout of the minutes to find out what decisions had been made. It took me eighteen months to get that changed."

"What the fuck? Did we fall back into the 1940s and I missed it?"

She chuckled, the sound dry and humorless. "Yeah. I guess I stayed because I thought I could make a difference. I don't mind fighting, and I was winning, you know?" She blew out a sigh. "Or at least I thought I was."

I waited, rolling the beer bottle between my palms, comfortable with the silence as Liv searched for more words.

"I quit. I realized there was nothing for me there anymore. So, I just up and quit."

I nodded, encouraging her to continue.

She ran a hand over her face. "I'm starting my own company. From here, in the Cape. I'll move back home, hire a cheap workspace, and we'll operate out of there for a while." Her lips twisted up into a small grin, some of the sparkle that she'd been missing reigniting.

"What about ye apartment?"

She laughed, shaking her head. "I think the universe is transpiring against me. My apartment's flooded. Some builders hit the main water pipe. The place is a write-off."

I winced. "Ouch. What a week, huh?"

"Yeah."

She fiddled with the label on her beer bottle, the silence suddenly awkward.

"So ye don't need to be in Rochester for filming?" I asked, referring to our country's version of LA.

She shook her head. "With documentaries, they can be filmed anywhere. It'll probably be good to set up an office further down the track, but in the meantime, the Cape will work. The local tax breaks are awesome, and I have a support network here for when the baby comes."

And there it is. The baby elephant in the room.

"Ah, the baby...." I sucked in a breath. "Are you keeping it?"

Liv's face flushed, but she nodded. "Are you angry?"

I shook my head. "Never, lass. Ye'll be a good mother. Great. I see how you are with your siblings. Bossing them about like a little mother hen. Ye'll love the little one fiercely."

She blew out a breath. "Thanks. What about you?"

"Me?" I blinked, eyebrows raising in surprise.

"Yeah. Will you love her or him?"

I scratched my chest, suddenly aware of the fact I still wasn't wearing a shirt. "Well... I guess. I mean, I love your brother's kids like they're my own."

The pinched expression on her face relaxed slightly. "And visitation? We'll have to work that out."

"Visit—" I broke off, a deadly chill freezing the blood in my veins. "Liv... are... are ye saying ye're pregnant with my babe?"

She frowned. "I thought... yes. Who else did you think—? "

Around me, the world began to sparkle, black dots winking in my vision.

"But... we used a condom," my protestation sounded weak and breathy as if I'd run up the side of a mountain at full steam.

"I think it must have been a dud. Or maybe you have super sperm? All I know is I haven't slept with anyone but you for over twelve months. Likely longer." She leaned forward, resting a hand on my arm. "Ian, you're the father."

And like that, my world blanked, my vision going black.

"Ian!"

CHAPTER 4

Liv

Well, *I hadn't planned for this scenario.*

I stood over Ian, staring down at the Sasquatch passed out on the kitchen floor. He'd crumbled slowly rather than fainting, so at least I didn't need to look for head injuries.

I leaned over, giving his hand a hard squeeze.

"Ian, wake up. Ian?"

He moaned, his eyes flickering open for a moment before they settled on my waist, then rolled back into his head, his body flopping back onto the floor once more.

The father of my child, ladies and gentlemen!

With a sigh, I found a pillow and blanket, propping his big head up and covering his half-naked form.

Now what?

This wasn't at all how I'd seen today going. The exhaustion I'd been fighting overtook me, the last of my adrenaline dissipating to leave behind a bone-aching weariness.

I looked at Ian's bed with its crumbled sheets and messy comforter. It invited me to sit a while and rest my weary head.

Maybe just for a moment. Just until Ian wakes.

With a groan, I sank onto the soft mattress, Ian's scent enveloping me.

Stupid Sasquatch.

I closed my eyes for a moment, finding the mixed scent of sawdust, cinnamon and clean laundry strangely comforting.

I'll close my eyes for a moment. Just a minute. Just... one... minute....

———

Ian

Why am I on the floor?

Not only was I on the floor, but I seemed to be lying in the kitchen, covered by a blanket with a pillow under my head. It took a moment for the memory of Liv's announcement to return.

Ah, ye shithead. You've royally cocked that up.

Did one normally faint at the news of their impending fatherhood? I couldn't recall any of my siblings mentioning this occurrence, but then they'd all been safely wedded before being bedded in a way that had resulted in progeny.

Fuck.

I pushed up from the floor, glancing at the clock above my bed, only for my gaze to stutter and halt on the woman curled around my remaining pillow.

For a tall, statuesque woman, she looked remarkably small and vulnerable in my bed, the dark circles around her eyes suddenly more pronounced in sleep.

On quiet feet, I gently pulled a blanket over her, then shuffled around the apartment, dressing as quietly as I could. I scribbled a note on a scrap of paper, dropping it on the kitchen counter before heading down into the warehouse.

"Morning," Erik called when I walked into the office. "Coffee's on."

My boss flipped through the mail, opening bills and muttering to himself as I poured a cup.

"Erik?"

"Mm?"

I hesitated, knowing this wasn't going to end well. "Liv is upstairs in the apartment. Rocked up early this morning."

Erik looked up from his papers. "Liv? As in my sister Liv?"

"Aye."

Erik frowned. "I'm sorry, I think I misheard. My sister is upstairs? As in upstairs in your apartment?"

I nodded, shuffling from foot to foot. "Arrived early this morning. Thought the apartment would be empty."

"Ah," Erik nodded, leaning back in his seat. "Is she coming down?"

I shook my head. "Poor lass passed out on my bed." I poured myself a splash of the coffee and took a sip, grimacing at the cheap brew. "Brother, ye need to up yer coffee game. This isn't fit for human consumption."

He tossed a pen my way, the tip hitting my

chest and bouncing to the floor. "Shut it, you bourgeois coffee snob."

"What can I say? Yer brother has ruined me for all time. The way Rune pours a cup...." I made a chef's kiss motion. "Bliss."

Erik laughed, shaking a finger in my direction. "I'll tell him you said that. I'm sure Gabby'll be pleased to know you're competing for his affections."

"Whose affections?" Gabby asked, walking through the door.

"Ye husband-to-be. That man can make a cup of coffee like no bodies business."

Gabby paused her hand on the coffee pot. "Did Erik make this?"

I nodded glumly, holding my mug up. "Tastes like Satan's ass."

"Hey!" Erik shoved up from the desk. "I know how to make coffee, okay? I just happen to like mine strong."

"Strong enough a damned spoon could stand in it," I muttered, grimacing again at the taste.

"Changing subject," Erik drawled, shooting me the bird. "Why is Liv passed out on your bed."

Gabby's head shot up. "Excuse me? Liv as in our Liv?"

I nodded, my heart doing a weird tap-dance as I attempted to skirt the issue.

"She caught the red eye. Doubt she meant to fall asleep, she just sat down for a moment and then passed out. Suspect she'll be out for a few hours."

Erik pulled his phone free, thumb scrolling across the screen. "She didn't post anything in the family chat."

"Didn't call us either," Gabby said, adding creamer and three packets of sugar to her strong-as-sin coffee. "Normally, we get a little advanced notice of when the whirlwind is arriving."

I cleared my throat, finding myself giving into the strangest sensation – a need to protect the mother of my child.

"Perhaps she wanted to surprise you." I crossed my arms, trying for a casual shrug. "It is nearly Thanksgiving, after all."

Gabby and Erik exchanged a look, then shrugged.

"Maybe," Erik said, looking back down at his paperwork.

"Alright, let's get to it."

Gabby led the way out the door, her coffee in hand. I trailed, glancing up at the apartment above the workshop where Liv still slept.

I have no idea what we're doing, but I'm not giving up my child without a fight.

With that decided, I got to work, trying to lose myself in the demanding physicality of the job I loved.

CHAPTER 5

Liv

I stared at myself in the mirror of Ian's bathroom.

Is that a bump?

I cupped my hands around my belly, giving it a little jiggle.

"Oh, God, it's a bump."

I reached for my phone and quickly googled *how many months before baby bump?*

Google, as always, had held the answers to life's mysteries.

You'll likely notice the first signs of a bump early in the second trimester, between weeks 12 and 16.

I did the sums, counting back to Gunnar's wedding.

"Thirteen weeks. Thirteen goddamned weeks." I looked down at my stomach, the tiny little pooch staring right back at me. "Well, we can't say you're not prompt. You must get that from me."

I'd known about the baby for less than twenty-four hours, and here I was, assigning traits to her.

Or him. Shit. When can I find out the sex? Is it possible to raise a baby gender-neutral? What does one call a gender-neutral child? Oh, God!

I spent the next hour sitting in a towel on the edge of the bathtub googling baby and parenthood questions.

"Liv?" Ian's voice floated through the door, a gentle tap following. "You in here?"

I yanked the door open, staring at the man who'd done this to me.

"You!"

His eyebrows went up, eyes widening as he took in my towel-clad body. "Um, are ye—"

"You did this to me!"

The man's face flushed. "I'd say it took two."

"Do you have any idea what kind of person it takes to raise a child in this day and age? I didn't!" I held up my phone. "Google tells me that good parents raise children that will positively contribute to society. I'M NOT A GOOD PARENT! I CAN'T DO THIS!"

He reached out, and I tried to dodge his hand, but the tiny bathroom severely limited my ability to maneuver. Ian snagged my arm, gently but deliberately pulling me into his chest. He wrapped me in a hug that felt all-encompassing, cradling me in such a way that I felt surrounded without feeling suppressed.

"Ye'll be a great mamma," he told me, his big hand cupping the back of my hair and gently stroking. "Ye love your little nephews fiercely. Ye'll do the same for this wee one. I've no doubt."

I nodded against his chest, my fingers clutching his plaid overshirt, the smell of woodchip, oil and soap both familiar and nostalgic. My father had smelt like Ian, my brothers, and my grandfather. I'd grown up around men who smelt like hard work and clean living. And it felt comforting to be embraced by someone who reminded me of all the men I loved in my life... even if I hated Ian with the fire of a billion suns.

"You good?" He asked after a long moment, his hand still gently caressing my hair.

"Yeah." I stepped back, hitching the towel, which had fallen slightly. "I should get dressed.

I need to eat, find a place to live, and announce to my family the baby situation."

Ian cleared his throat. "Ye're planning on keeping it then?"

My eyebrows rose, my temper flaring, any goodwill gone. "Of course, I'm keeping it! Do you think I'm this conflicted about parenting because I'm planning something else?"

He held his hands up in a pacifying gesture. "Your body, yer rules. I'm not here to judge, lass. I'm here to help no matter what options you choose. And thankfully, unlike some, you do have options. And support. And a man who's willing to do whatever necessary to support you and the wee one."

That took some of the heat out of my temper.

"Thank you. I appreciate that." I forced myself to calm down. "I know abortion is a viable option but...." I pressed a had to my stomach. "I want them. Whoever they are."

Ian lifted his big hand, cupping my cheek. "So tell me what ye need right now."

"Pie."

He pulled back a little at the same time it hit me what I'd just asked for.

"Pie?"

I nodded, my stomach grumbling. "Yeah, actually. Pie."

The nausea that had hovered at the edges of my conscious for the past few months suddenly evaporated, my mouth actually watering as I thought about pie.

Pregnant.

No job.

No home.

This definitely called for pie.

"Pie. Right. What type? Pumpkin? Lime? Pecan?"

"Yes. And chocolate."

Ian cocked an eyebrow. "Sorry, did you just want the chocolate?"

"No, bring me all of them."

Ian tilted his head in my direction as if he hadn't quite heard me. "All...?"

I nodded, rubbing my little bump. "And cherry. Oh, any blueberry if they have it? Actually, give me five minutes to get dressed, and I'll come with you. We can hit up Cathy's Bakery."

I made a move to stand, but Ian clapped a hand on my shoulder, keeping me in place.

"Stay. I'll get your pie. Just get decent, and I'll be back."

He left, shutting the door, leaving me with a rumbling tummy and a baby bump.

Story of my fucking life.

CHAPTER 6

Ian

Liv wasn't kidding about the pies. The woman hoovered them down them with the enthusiasm of a rabid Labrador.

"Ye want to slow down?" I asked as she finished her second pie and began reaching for the third.

"Um, you want to shut your pie hole?" she retorted, pulling the bakery box to her and lifting the lid. "I have hardly eaten in months. This baby wants pie? This baby gets pie."

I shook my head, watching her scoop up a giant chunk of cherry filling. "Are you really blaming our unborn baby for yer need to inhale pie?"

She paused, fork hovering just in front of her lips. "Is this really a conversation you want to be having, Ian?"

Sensing I was far out of my depth I kept my mouth shut.

"Good choice." She moaned as the cherry coated bite disappeared between her lips, her eyelids drifting close, her head tipping back to savor the taste.

Unbidden and unwelcome memories surfaced.

Liv bent over the bed. My hand fisted in her hair, drawing her head back to bear her neck for me to taste. Pressing hot, hungry kisses along her throat. Nipping at her as my cock—

Pull it together man!

My cock didn't get the message. The traitor stiffened, pulsing in angry protest when I made no attempt to reach across the table and kiss Liv.

She's pregnant, ye filthy bugger. Settle down.

She may be pregnant, but she ain't dead... neither are you.

"Does Erik know I'm up here?"

Liv pulled me from my thoughts.

"Aye."

"What did you tell him?"

I shrugged. "Nothing about you or the babe beyond that you're here."

"And your reasons for being here and supplying me with pie?"

"Just that I was taking a half-day. I've worked overtime the last few weeks on a project or two, and ye know we set our own times around here."

She nodded; her mouth full of cherry pie.

I bet she tastes delicious.

I shoved that way, locking it in a dungeon in the recesses of my mind.

Jesus, this is the Harpy, remember?

I remember the way her mouth felt when she—

"So when are we telling your parents the news?" I asked, my gut pinching.

Liv stopped chewing, her nose wrinkling as she swallowed. "Ah, about that."

"I suspect it'll be hard to keep the bump hidden in another month or so."

She blew out a breath. "So, here's the thing... I've been thinking."

Uh-oh.

"We should probably tell them tonight. But if they suspect for even a moment that we're not in love, it's going to be hell."

I coughed, choking on air. "Sorry, did you say in *love*?"

She nodded, forking another bite of cherry pie. "You know my parents, and Nan, for that matter. They'll accept anything so long as it includes love."

"But... they all know we hate each other."

She cocked her eyebrow at me, her fork held at a jaunty angle. "I'd say this baby bump proves otherwise."

I swallowed, attempting to get moisture back into my mouth. "You want me to pretend."

She nodded. "At least until the baby's born. Then we can say that we parted amicably."

"And the wee one?"

She hesitated, chewing for a long moment. "That depends. How involved do you want to be?"

My gaze dropped to the tiny swell of her belly, and I felt something I'd never experienced before. A strange mixture of fierce protection, abject fear, and a love so strong I knew I'd die with it burning in my gut.

"At a push? A hundred and ten percent."

She sighed, finally discarding the fork, one hand unconsciously resting on her stomach. "I thought so."

"You have an issue with that?"

She shook her head. "No, just complicates things. I'm prepared to raise our baby alone.

You being in the picture makes this simultaneously harder and easier."

"Because of your job?"

She nodded, then shook her head. "Yes and no. If you're keen, then I want our child to have even time with their parents. But shared parenting also means we need to be on the same page about their upbringing."

"Alright, let's work through it." I reached for a slice of cherry pie, noting Liv's eyes narrowed as she watched me spoon it onto my plate.

Greedy wench.

"Do you have pen and paper?"

I waved a hand towards the kitchenette. "I'm sure somewhere in there."

"In that case, I'll use my phone. That way, I can email you a copy."

I hid a smile, amused that Liv thought a twenty-minute conversation followed by a no doubt well-crafted email could solve all our problems.

"Oh! Google has a questionnaire available." She looked up, grinning. "You ready for us to work out how different we are?"

"Not sure we need a quiz to tell us that but go on."

"Okay, what religion should we raise the baby?"

My eyebrows lifted. "I didn't take you for a God-fearing type."

"I'm not. But my family is… Lutheran? Pentecostal?" She shrugged. "Something like that. I'm sure Mom will want them to know that side."

I nodded. "We're Catholic, born and raised. But I have no particular ties to it." The palm of my hand gave an involuntary twitch, a reminder of school-boy punishments dished out by the head Nun.

"Let's say Christian, then."

"Works for me."

She made a note on her phone. "Oh, should we call your parents?"

A bitterness twisted in my gut. "We can announce after we tell your family. Let's just see how that goes first."

Liv nodded, absently flicking a chunk of hair from her face. "I'll admit, I don't remember ever meeting your parents."

Good.

"Aye, it's rare they come out to America. Ye've met Mam, though it was a fleeting visit."

"How many siblings do you have?"

"Eight. Last I checked."

She laughed as if it were a joke. "Wow, your house must have been a riot growing up."

Not quite.

I nodded vaguely. "Next question?"

Liv looked down at her phone, reading, "bottle or breast?"

"Uh, I suspect that's up to you, lass."

She shook her head, scrunching up her nose. "Bottle means you can take her overnight. Breast means she'll have to stay with me full-time for the first few months."

"But what do ye want?" I asked softly, watching her face carefully.

A naked longing crossed her face before it was wiped clear.

Breast it is then.

"Maybe... I mean... if you don't mind—"

"Pop breast down on your list. We'll make it work."

"Are you sure?"

I nodded, watching as a small pleased blush colored her cheeks. "Next question?"

"Vaccinations?"

I blanched. "That bloody well better be a trick question."

She laughed, typing on the screen. "Pro-vaccines. Agreed. How about discipline?"

"I don't believe in hitting."

"Good, neither do I." She gave me an approving look. "Circumcision?"

My cock, which had remained at half-mast

through this entire conversation, shrivelled. "Not a fan of genital mutilation."

"Good, neither am I."

"Photos online?"

I crossed my arms, bracing for a battle. "No. No baby of mine is having a digital footprint before they can even walk."

"Um, agreed." Liv raised an eyebrow. "Why is this so easy?"

No idea.

"Raising the child?" She asked.

"Well that should be easy. We're both in the Cape for now. And when we get to the point that changes then we'll make decisions together."

Liv raised a hand, nibbling absently on her thumbnail. "Speaking of, I'm going to need to find a house. Or at least an apartment."

The words rolled off my tongue before I could think better of it. "No, ye won't. You'll move in with me."

Silence dominated the room, Liv staring at me with her big blue eyes.

In the pause, I took her in. She'd showered, her hair now slightly damp but clean, the blonde shiny and soft looking. She'd dressed casually, jeans and a navy-blue t-shirt, but still managed to look like a million dollars.

"Move in with you?" She repeated, her

hand now rubbing her stomach. "Why would I do that?"

"I... I want the full experience."

God, it feels weird to say admit.

Liv's eyebrows, already lifted, surged a fraction higher. "I'm sorry?"

"I want to see ye get round with our babe. I want to rub your ankles when they're swollen and go with you to the appointments. I wanna be there for you, Liv. And when our babe is older and going through this themselves – if they choose to – then I want to have that point of reference. I want to be the man, the father, they'd expect me to be from the verra moment I knew of them."

My voice had grown thick, emotion clogging my throat.

"But you don't even like me," she pointed out as if that changed anything.

"I like you. Ye just niggle me the wrong way sometimes."

She blanched. "I... what? No, I don't."

"Aye, ye do." I pointed a forkful of pie in her direction. "You're constantly hen-pecking me, making me out to be some kind of neanderthal as if I've not a brain in my head."

"I know you have a brain. It's the rest of you that's the issue."

My eyebrows rose, surprise coloring my reaction. "You want to explain more?"

She waved a hand dismissively. "You know what you did."

"What *I* did?"

What the devil is she on about?

"Yeah, that first year."

I tried to remember, wracking my brain and coming up empty. "Ye're gonna have to enlighten me."

"Wait, you really don't remember?"

I shook my head, completely mystified by this turn of events.

"Ian." Liv's big blue eyes searched my face, her cheeks flushing with anger. "Please tell me you're joking."

Something lit in my gut, a rough kind of anticipation.

"Tell me."

"You... you...." Liv slapped a hand on the tabletop, practically vibrating with rage. "You idiot! I got drunk one night, and you happened to be in the bar. I was home for the holidays and blowing off steam. Remember that?"

A hazy memory came to me, Liv in a low-cut dress, her ass practically hanging out while her breasts bounced enticingly. She'd been young, wild, and carefree. I'd been young, wild, and far too randy.

"You freaking hauled me over your shoulder, took me out to the parking lot and spanked me! Spanked, Ian! Like I was two freaking years old. Then you called my brothers to come pick me up as if I were some naughty child and not an adult. You were completely out of line!"

A newer memory transferred itself onto my conscious, clinging greedily as I listened to Liv rage.

My cock fucking Liv with wild abandon. Liv under me, squirming, panting, desperate. The clench of her. The feel. Years of frustration, annoyance, and attraction channelled into mind-fucking pleasure.

Liv pushed to her feet, beginning to pace, her hands waving wildly in agitation.

My hand curved around her throat, my palm still hot from spanking her ass. Her resistance followed by her sweet submission.

My cock hardened, pressing against my zipper.

Kiss her.

I pushed up, stalking across the small space to back Liv against the wall. She stared at me with wide eyes, any anger momentarily wiped from her expression.

"What are you doing?"

"What's it look like, ye daft lass? I'm kissing

ye." I leaned down, my lips a bare whisper from hers, when hands slapped into my chest, forcing me back a step.

"Uh-uh. No way, bucko. Thanks for the offer, but no thanks. The last time we kissed, I ended up pregnant. This—" she gestured between us, "—it ain't happening."

Masculine sexual outrage lit my blood, the need to prove her wrong nearly overwhelming.

You're not that kind of man. Get a hold of yourself.

I pulled back, physically turning away from her, fighting with my control, reigning in the desire to imprint my body upon this woman.

"I'm sorry," I said finally, turning back around to face her. "For then and now. I'm sorry I was a neanderthal and made ye feel less. You're not, Liv. You never have been. You're a talented, beautiful woman. If anything, I wanted ye to be mine back then and was likely sloshed myself that night. And I'm sorry for now. For getting ye pregnant and for wanting to kiss ye. I'm not sorry for the babe, could never be, but I'm sorry for the complication I've added."

For a moment, Liv just looked at me, her expression shuttered. A heartbeat passed, and as I watched, she crumpled, her body bowing in, her face falling as she began to sob as if her world were ending.

"Ooch, come here." I hauled her into my arms and into a chair, slightly concerned at its ability to hold our combined weight as it groaned in protest under us.

"Y-y-you can't be nice to me one minute and a complete dickhead the next! It's not fair!" she wailed, one fist pounding at my chest. "Not when I'm unemployed, homeless and pregnant! I've never been even *one* of those! This is really hard!"

She cried, and I let her, listening and making soothing noises. She needed to let it out, purge herself of grief and stress.

It took a while but finally she quietened, the only sound little hitches of her breath and the occasional hiccup.

"We'll get through this," I promised, cupping her head and pressing a kiss to her crown.

"Yeah."

Her soft agreement warmed me, giving me hope.

Perhaps we can make this work.

CHAPTER 7

Liv

I'd had an afternoon nap, my first since leaving the age of toddler-hood behind. I felt strangely refreshed and ready to take on the world.

Perhaps I should have napped more often in my life.

I'd rallied the troops, group texting the family to assemble for dinner at Erik's house. Gunnar and Ella would be video calling in as they were in Capricorn Cove spending the holidays with her family this year.

Good luck to them, they're gonna need it.

Having met Ella's brothers, I could categorically say that the Bronze's made my family look practically angelic.

I tugged at my dress, sighing at the noticeable bump that stretched the material.

No hiding it. I'm definitely pregnant.

"Worried?" Ian asked from beside me in the cab of his truck.

"No. Just wanting to get it over with."

"And you're a hundred percent sure ye want to go through with this charade?" Ian asked as he turned into my parent's street.

I nodded, pressing damp palms to the material across my thighs. "It's the only option that doesn't leave my mother in tears of worry."

Ian parked the truck smoothly, twisting to look at me. "Ye forget, I know your mother. The woman will worry no matter what."

My mother was both a warrior and a worrier, the combination making her a fierce protector of her family. I vowed to be just like her.

"Let's just get this over with."

We exited the truck, my arms full of pie, Ian carrying pizzas. It wasn't the most glamorous dinner, but considering I'd thrust myself upon Erik and Laura, it was the least I could do.

We let ourselves in, Ian's big voice booming a welcome.

"Anyone home?" he called, leading the way.

Laura's head poked from around the hall door, a welcoming smile on her lips. "Hey, Ian. Oh, and Liv! Hi. Come on in, we're just in the kitchen."

My brother owned a large house on one of the canals. It suited him. A jetty out the back for whichever boat he'd designed for himself that month, a big house he and Laura would no doubt fill with children.

Perhaps one of the best decisions I'd ever made had been to sign Laura Sweep as my reality TV Queen of Clean. She'd not only helped me create a show with heart and soul, scoring us both an Emmy and a GLAAD, but through the show, she'd also met my brother. Their romance had played out like a choreographed love story, the reality TV show host falling for the adorably clueless single dad of adopted twin boys.

Truly, I couldn't have written it any better.

"Liv! All this fuss for your homecoming." My mother approached, wrapping me in her arms, her familiar perfume reducing me to a five-year-old, clinging to her for reassurance.

"Mom," I greeted, closing my eyes and holding her just a little tighter, a little longer.

She let go, stepping back to cup my cheeks, searching my face. "What's wrong?"

"Is everyone here?"

"No, but Rune and Gabby are on their way, and Dad and Nan are picking up Astrid from the store," Erik replied, gently shifting Mom out of his way to give me a one-armed hug. "Hey, sis."

"Hey, you." I embraced him, circling both him and the baby in his arm. "And you, Mister Ulf."

Ulf, my gorgeous nephew, chortled happily, his little hands clapping.

"You're so big!" I exclaimed, pressing exuberant kisses to his cheek, delighting in his baby laughter.

"Don't remind me, he's starting to cruise now. It's terrifying. We're in a mad dash to install baby gates," Laura said, Leif, my other nephew, balanced on her hip.

"Hey, babe." She leaned in, pressing a kiss to my cheek as we hugged.

"So, where are Dad and Nan?" I asked as we crowded around the kitchen island.

"Your sister came home early from college. She's staying at the house and working at the bookstore." Mom shook her head. "There's something going on with that girl, and she won't reveal a word."

"She's young," Erik dismissed, bustling around the kitchen to remove cups and place them on the counter. "She's probably just burned out from a hectic college year."

Mom shook her head, her blonde hair, now faded to a silvery grey, flying about.

"Liv, she dyed her hair. Brown! It's a nice brown, but still. When has your sister ever dyed her hair? It's like she's rebelling, and I have no idea why."

I exchanged an amused look with Laura, who dipped her head, hiding behind her own long brunette strands, her shoulders shaking as she struggled not to laugh. My whole family were blonde-headed, Viking giants. Tall, and broad, we reflected Dad's Nordic heritage. Mom, while golden blonde, had the stature of a small Madonna, coming up only to my father's armpit. That she took Astrid's decision to change up her look as a personal rejection of the family didn't surprise me. Mom was nothing, if not a little dramatic.

"Now Jemma," Ian tutted, shaking his shaggy head. "Ye know yer daughter well enough. She's not the kind to brood in silence. She seems happy enough."

Mom nodded, patting Ian on the arm. "You're a treasure, Ian. But a mother always knows when something is bothering her children."

She sent me a side eye, and I swallowed,

nausea rising as my stomach began to roil with nerves.

"We're here!" Gabby, my youngest brother's fiancé, stepped through the door, a bottle of wine held in each hand. Gabby had to be one of my favorite people alive. Fierce, loving, and unashamed, I'd never met a woman who was so simultaneously vulnerable and bold.

An aquamarine choker decorated her neck, matching the color of her new prosthetic leg.

"Hello!" she gushed, wrapping me in a hug, a bottle digging into my back. "Don't you look wonderful."

She smelled like sawdust, coconut and salt, the combination a result of her perfume and occupation.

"And hello to you, Ms Former Apprentice," I greeted, pleased as punch for her. "I hope my brother gave you a pay rise to go with that shiny new title."

She cackled, shooting Erik, who also happened to be her boss, a wink. "A small one, but we're still negotiating."

My brother's eyebrows lifted. "The fuck we are. You may be family, but girl, you're not getting any preferential treatment."

Gabby's arms were replaced by Rune's solid form. He lifted me up, squeezing me tight.

My youngest sibling was the gentle (but massive) giant of the family.

"Rune put me down." I laughed, squirming a little. He did, pressing a quick kiss to my forehead before trailing his fiancé through the house.

"Your family love hard and fierce," Ian commented, handing me a glass of something sparkling.

"And loud," I agreed, sniffing at the contents.

"Lemonade. For the... nerves," he said softly, glancing at the gathering group.

"Thanks."

Dad and Nan arrived a moment later, Nan seated like a queen in her wheelchair.

"Hello, darling." She kissed my cheek, patting my hair as I bent to hug her. "You've been missed."

Dad followed, though he was so quickly distracted by Mom pestering him about opening the wine that his greeting was nothing more than a fleeting squeeze.

Astrid hovered in the doorway; her cheeks flushed as she stared at the family.

"Are you here for me?" she asked as I started towards her, her mouth a thin line.

"Nope, but nice hair. The color suits you."

I pulled her into my arms, holding her tight. "You okay?"

She stood stiff in my arms for a moment, her body tense, stress written in every line. Slowly she melted, her arms squeezing me back. "Yeah. I'm just working things through, you know?"

I nodded, letting my hug do all the talking. Of my siblings, Gunnar was the oldest, then came Erik, me, Astrid and finally, Rune. I'd always thought my sister would become a teacher. But instead, she was in her final semester of a masters in Architecture, a field she'd never expressed an interest in before heading off to College to pursue. It hadn't made any sense then and didn't now, but I wasn't one to question another's life choices.

Well, not unless I thought those life choices warranted interference.

"Dinner?" Ian asked the crowd as they mingled.

"Yes." Mom decided, picking up plates. "Sune, get the napkins, Rune, help Ian with the pizzas. Liv, can you bring Nan?"

"I can bring myself!" Nan yelled, pressing the joystick to send her chair into movement.

Astrid chuckled, one arm wrapped around my middle as we followed the rabble out to the back patio. Space heaters and a cheerfully crackling fire kept the cold night air at bay as we crowded around the table, serving up pizza and laughing at each other. Erik handed Ulf off to Ian, disappearing inside to return with a small laptop.

"Hi, family!" Ella called, waving through the screen. My eldest brother sat beside her, a beer in one hand, his other arm around his bride.

Possessive thy name is Gunnar.

As everyone settled, greeting Ella and Gunnar, and chatting as pizzas were eaten and drinks sipped, I swallowed against the nausea, staring at the single slice of pizza on my plate.

I want pie.

My mouth watered at the thought. Cherry, apple, chocolate, it didn't matter. I wanted pie, Goddamn it!

I felt eyes on me, lifting my gaze to see Ian staring at me across the table. He still looked like a Sasquatch, with his explosion of red hair and out-of-control beard. But I found myself looking past that exterior, seeing him through new eyes.

He still held Ulf, who tugged at Ian's beard, Ian ignoring him to watch me. He'd greeted my family with the familiarity of a man invited to many of these events. He fit in, teasing Laura, niggling Ian, and helping Mom. He and Dad regularly shared a beer, raging about the local football team.

He fits.

I sucked in a breath, looking away from Ian's piercing gaze to the table. They'd quieted a little while eating, the dim the perfect time to raise my news. With a deep breath, I stood, lifting my glass and holding it out.

"I have an announcement," I declared, determined to make this a good thing. "Actually, I have a few, and I hope you'll celebrate with me."

Worried glances were exchanged around the table.

"Go on, Liv," Gunnar encouraged through the screen. "Tell us."

"I...." I swallowed, taking the easy out. "I quit my job. I'm moving back to the Cape and starting my own company. We're going to make feature films and documentaries."

The table exploded, congratulations, hugs, cheers. My family didn't question my decision, they simply supported me a hundred percent.

I met Ian's gaze across the table, Ulf still in the crook of his arm, the toddler still fascinated with his beard.

"Thank you," I said as they began to settle down. "And I have another announcement."

"Two in one day? How exciting!" Mom called, giving me a thumbs up.

Oh, Mother, you sweet, innocent lady. I hope this doesn't destroy you.

Determined, I lifted my glass, bracing for the inevitable impact. "Ian and I are together, and we're having a baby."

Silence.

Deathly, fucking silence.

My nephews picked up on the vibe, their little heads swirling to look around the table. Ulf stuck a fist in his mouth, urgently sucking while Leif began to fuss in Laura's arms, his tiny face screwing up, ready to begin screaming.

This does not bode well.

"I fucking knew it!" Ella exploded, her body bouncing up and down on the screen. "I told you! It happened at the wedding, didn't it? You got together at our wedding!"

"Umm... yes?"

She laughed, turning to punch Gunnar's arm. "I told you! I said there was something there. That dance." She fanned herself, shaking her head. "Phew! I nearly got pregnant just watching you two."

"Pregnant? Are you sure?" Erik asked, his expression shell-shocked.

I rolled my eyes. "Do you think I'd look this bloated for fun?"

"But you hate each other," Erik said, beginning to shake his head back and forth slowly. "You do nothing but fight."

"Hate and love, the gap between both is narrow," Astrid offered eyeing my belly. "Perhaps it wasn't so much hate as...."

"Foreplay?" Gabby offered with a laugh.

"Are you sure you're pregnant?" Mom asked tears in her eyes. "Have you done the test? Seen a doctor?"

"Test yes, doctor no. But we're sure. I've all the signs, and every test from the first to the twenty-first came back positive."

"Oh, Livvy!" Mom threw herself across the table, scrambling to come and wrap me in a hug. "My babies are having babies!"

Across the table, I saw Dad offering Ian a handshake, clapping him enthusiastically on the back.

"To Liv and Ian!" Gunnar called, toasting.

"To Liv and Ian!" my family echoed, laughing and clinking glasses.

Ian reached across the table, tapping his beer against my glass. "To our baby."

I drank, my eyes never leaving his as around us, the questions began to fly thick and fast.

He toasted our baby.
Well shit. Now I have to like him.

CHAPTER 8

Ian

I rolled, trying not to wince as the tiny couch protested under my weight. The clock from the microwave blinked at me with its too bright digits.

1 am and I had yet to catch a wink.

From the bed across the room I heard Liv give a soft sigh, the bed clothes shifting as she turned in her sleep.

Whose idea was this again? Oh right, mine.

Dinner had gone well. Surprisingly so. We'd played the adoring couple, falling into an easy rhythm of give and take. Having called this temporary truce, Liv and I could apparently get along without niggling each other. The banter was still there, don't get me wrong. But it felt softer, less antagonizing and more... affectionate?

I frowned, replaying tonight in my head.

Yeah, affectionate seemed the right word. No one overly drilled us on our relationship, and we kept details vague but her family didn't mind, more interested in finding out what we'd need for the baby and what our plans were – Sune in particular had been very interested in understanding if I had any marriage-minded plans for his precious daughter.

Like she'd even say yes.

Jesus, Ian. What are ye thinking man? Marriage?

Sleep had obviously deserted me. With a sigh, I reached for my phone, searching for eBooks to read while waiting for dawn to arrive.

What to expect when you're expecting.

The Expectant Father.

Being a Dad is Weird.

The Feminist Guide to Daddy-ing.

I hit download, beginning to flick through.

So, you wanna be a dad. Well brother, strap in. We're about to go on a hell of a journey.

"Ian?"

I blinked, looking up from my phone, pulled back from my reading haze by Liv. She stood before me, a cup of tea in one hand, toast in the other, holding them out to me.

My mind swirled with all the facts and advice, an uncomfortable sense of overwhelm hitting me.

"Oh, morning." I dropped the phone, reaching for the crockery. "Is this for me?"

She laughed, nodding, her face still flushed from sleep. She wore a loose robe, the thick material protecting her from the cold.

"Yes, you look like you need it."

"Thanks." I took a long sip, finding she'd made my tea just how I liked it, strong with a dash of milk. "How'd ye know this is how I take it?"

She shrugged, returning to the fridge and beginning to rummage through the shelves. "I listen." She poked her head out. "Do you know where the other pie is? All I can find is apple."

Shit.

"Ah, I might have eaten it."

She reared up, narrowing her eyes on me. "Excuse me?'"

I winced. "I got hungry."

"You got... Ian! What am I meant to do now?"

With a sigh, I pushed to my feet. "Eat the apple. I'll get dressed and go get you some more."

My back protested, reminding me that I couldn't do another night on the couch.

Monday can't come quick enough.

Liv smashed angrily around the kitchen, banging and clanging before shaking a giant can of whipped cream. Her gaze met mine, her eyes flashing with rage as she began to spray cream on the pastry.

One swirl, two, three.

"Do ye think you have enough?" I asked, staring as she continued to hold the button down.

"No."

Frustration lit in me as I watched her add more cream. "You'll make yourself sick. Stop."

"I will not. Don't tell me what to do to."

With a curse, I stalked across the kitchen, snatching for the can, Liv pulling back to avoid my reach. An arc of cream flew through the air covering counter, me and the ceiling.

"Look what you did!"

"Me?" I roared. "You're the idiot with the cream fetish!"

"It's not a fetish! It's what the baby wants!"

"The baby isn't old enough to know what it wants! She's only just getting taste buds!"

Liv froze, her eyes widening. "What?"

I paused, my anger banking. "Taste buds develop at around thirteen weeks. When she tastes the amniotic fluid, she'll get a wee sample of your diet."

Liv's hands dropped to her stomach; the fight forgotten. "You keep calling it her."

As do you.

I shrugged, all my anger dissipating. "I've no doubt you're birthing another heathen woman to bring hellfire and brimstone down upon the heads of any man stupid enough to underestimate her. Now, stop with the cream and let me get you another pie."

I turned, heading to the closet to get some clothes.

"Ian?"

"Yeah?"

"Just saying, if you'd tried again, I'd have let you kiss me just now."

I turned, grinning.

"Oh really?"

Liv's face had flushed, a small grin on her lips, one hand resting on her belly. She'd never looked more beautiful.

Stop before you get feelings.

"Yeah. But you know...." She shrugged. "I still hate you." There was no heat in her tone.

I laughed, turning away from her, my heart lighter. "I know, now eat your pie."

CHAPTER 9

Liv

I'd officially moved in with Ian. Ian and I were living together.

God that sounds weird.

The weekend had passed in a whirlwind of activity, Ian buying me pie, both of us googling a hundred different things about babies.

We'd briefly gone shopping to look at strollers, and baby carriers, and cradles—all the detritus that came with a new born.

Things I now knew– tiny booties made me hyperventilate. And Ian was damned good at soothing me through a panic attack.

I stood staring at the room that Ian had given me, the bed we'd picked up today, my things I'd unpacked. It felt... strange. Wrong.

Uncomfortable. As if I were a puzzle piece in the wrong box.

I should be sleeping with Ian.

"Ye ready?"

I jerked upright, twisting to find the man in question standing in the doorway to my bedroom, jeans molded to his legs, shirt pulled tight across his chest.

I want to ride him like a pony.

"Liv?"

I snapped to, hyper aware of the fact my underwear felt damn, my body throbbing with desire.

A man buys me pie and moves me into his house and I'm ready to jump his bones.

"Yep, let's do this." I picked up my tote, allowing him to lead us out. We chatted as he drove us down town to the doctor's office where I'd have my first scan.

At reception, I filled in the clipboard handing it back as butterflies began to take flight.

"You okay?"

I nodded, my hand finding his, linking our fingers. "Just nervous. I've never been a mom before."

He chuckled, nodding at the other pregnant women in the waiting room. "I suspect the doctor knows what she's doing."

"Ms. Larsson?"

I stood, Ian's hand still reassuringly gripping mine. "Here."

"Come on through." The nurse led us through the offices to a small room at the back. A woman of indeterminant age stood inside, a friendly grin on her face.

"Hi Liv, I'm Dr. Kristen Lowe, take a seat."

We settled, Ian still allowing me to death grip his hand.

"Now, let me have a look at this file. This is your first, yes?"

I nodded, struck mute by the equipment in the room, and intimidated by this competent woman.

"They're always fun. Congratulations." She flicked through the chart I'd filled out, reading the info. "Says here you think the date of conception is 15 August? That's very specific."

I nodded, swallowing. "We're long-distance. It was the only opportunity."

She nodded. "Alright, and no blood test?"

I shook my head. "No, we didn't even think we were pregnant until last week."

"That's no problem. We'll do an ultrasound today just to confirm there is a baby but everything I'm seeing here is good so let's have a little peek and see what we have."

She helped me onto the bed, then asked me to lift my shirt and pull down my pants a little. I did so, shuffling around as she got the equipment ready.

"Okay, sorry, it'll feel cool and sticky for a little while thanks to the gel but let's see what we've got."

I reached out, clinging to Ian, fear pounding through me.

Oh, God, what if I'm wrong? What if there is no baby?

She moved the sensor around, spreading the gel. For a moment nothing appeared on the screen then I saw it, a teeny tiny head.

Ian's hand jerked in mine, crushing my fingers.

"There we go, hello baby," Kristen said with a grin, moving the sensor around. "Now let me see if I can..." she touched some buttons and a thumping sound filter through the speakers. "There. That's your baby's heartbeat. Congratulations."

Tears sprang to my eyes, sliding down my cheeks. Ian leaned in; his beard rough against my cheek.

"Congratulations, Mom."

I looked at him, our gazes meeting and holding, his eyes glassy with tears.

"And to you, Daddy."

He laughed, his teeth flashing, skin flushing with pleasure. "Now there's a thought. Me, a Dad? Crazy."

I chuckled, turning back to watch the screen avidly, our baby beginning to move just a little at all the poking and prodding.

Ian cleared his throat. "Can ye print that out? I'd like a copy for our mantel. Our babe's first picture."

"Of course," Kristen replied grinning. "It's always nice when the partners are this invested."

I love Ian.

The thought hit me, unbidden and unwelcome, rejection immediately following on its heels.

No, I don't.

It had to be the pregnancy hormones. I didn't just fall in love with a Sasquatch over a weekend. No way no how.

"Definitely around that thirteen to fourteen-week mark, so your timing checks out. We're too early for sex if you wanted to know. But come back after the holidays and we'll do the twenty-week scan, make sure everything is as it should be and, if you want, we can find out the sex then."

"I want," I told her, looking up at Ian. "That okay?"

"Fine by me."

She took more measurements and scans, checking everything out before letting me clean up. I left with a referral for a blood test, some vitamins, a list of local pre-natal and parents' classes, and a pamphlet as thick as my arm on birthing options.

And three little printouts of the scan. Baby's first picture.

"Should we call your parents now?" I asked, staring down at the image of our little one as Ian drove us home.

"Uh...." He cleared his throat. "If you wish."

Wait. What?

I twisted in my seat, giving him an eyebrow lift. "I'm sorry, if I wish? This coming from the man who asked for pictures of our unborn child? Alright, buddy, spill. What the fuck?"

He ran a hand over his face, his shoulders slumping. "This calls for alcohol."

My eyebrows lifted. "Excuse me?"

"Let me get a beer and something to eat, and we can talk."

I glanced at the dash clock; it was barely after eleven in the morning. "Ian...."

"Please, Liv."

I bit my tongue, struggling against my initial reaction to demand answers.

"Fine," I said finally. "The Literary Academy is open, and Rune might be willing to part with a beer at this time of the day. If you're lucky."

With that decided, he hit the indicator, navigating the streets towards Rune's establishment while I wondered what exactly I was getting myself into.

CHAPTER 10

Ian

The Literary Academy had been around for more than twenty years. Passed down in the Larsson family, Rune had taken it over when Nan had gotten too old. The kid had revamped it, popping out one side of the building and taking over the adjacent warehouse. He'd turned one part into a café-by-day-tapas-bar-by-night deal, with the other the original bookstore. But he'd revamped that too, creating a wonderland with fantasy-inspired sculptures made entirely from old books, delighting readers and becoming a photography mecca for social media influencers.

That Rune got free publicity from the

social media darlings hadn't gone unnoticed, the guy capitalized on that shit like no bodies business.

With a strange sense of foreboding we entered the café finding it in the mid-morning, just before lunch, lull.

We found a small booth set off from the book tunnel, tucked away for privacy. Liv set her bag down, ordering a small hot chocolate, unwinding her scarf from around her neck and pulling off her mittens.

"Can I get a beer?" I asked, praying for luck.

The waiter blinked. "Um... no. Sorry. But Rune might be able to do an Irish coffee?"

"That'll do."

"Actually, do you have pie?" Liv asked, catching the waiter before he moved off.

"Yeah, we've got pumpkin, rhubarb and strawberry, custard, or peach."

"Um, yes, please." Liv moaned, licking her lips. "One slice of each, thanks."

The guy's eyebrows raised but to his credit he took the order, shuffling away.

"Alright, Campbell. Hit me."

I reached for a sugar packet, needing to do something with my hands. "Let's wait 'til your pie arrives, I don't want to be interrupted."

Liv's lips pressed into a thin line, her blue

eyes flashing with annoyance. But she did as asked, waiting until the pies and drinks were delivered.

She picked up a fork stabbing it viciously into one of the pies. "Now talk."

I took a hearty sip of the coffee, embracing the alcoholic kick.

Now or never.

"My father is both an alcoholic and an adulterer. I have eight siblings because most are half-siblings. The man is still married to Mam, and she knows about the children but turns a blind eye, such is her love for the no-good son of a bitch."

Liv winced. "Damn. That sucks."

I nodded, running a tired hand over my face. "Aye, and it gets worse. For many a year, he took me along, using me as an excuse. Play dates with the local kids, he said while stepping out, taking advantage. By the time I realized, Mam had already found out and shrunk in on herself, deciding it wasn't in her best interest to do anything about it."

I looked up, finding Liv's gaze on me. "I hate him, Liv. For what he did to her. For what he did to all the women. Telling them he loved them. Leading them on. Knocking them up. I'm the eldest and have eight half-siblings – and they're the ones we know about."

"He must pay child support, surely."

"Aye, that he does."

"God, that must ruin him."

And now for the shitty part.

I cleared my throat, scratching at my beard nervously. "Not quite. You see, we're... um... that is to say..."

Spit it out Campbell!

"My father is a laird. A duke. He's got a massive holding in Scotland. We're what you call well-heeled."

Liv's eyes bugged out, her jaw dropping. "I'm sorry, did you say a duke? You mean you're royalty?"

I shook my head. "Not to the Brits. Our bloodline is pure Scot. Well, it was 'til this little one." I nodded at her belly. "But we're aristocracy."

She sucked in a breath, putting two and two together, such a clever lass.

"It's why you were able to move to America at seventeen," she whispered, her face draining of color. "You had a fallback."

"Aye. Nan and Mum were sad to see me go, but they knew I couldn't stay. I couldn't sit back and watch Dad play her like that. Not again."

"And the degrees?" she asked, referring to my multiple university titles.

"Paid for from my trust fund. Thought I'd

better put at least some of it to good use, even if I only use them when drunk women need to be bailed out of jail."

The reminder of her drunken shenanigans at Ella's bachelorette party didn't even get a flicker.

Liv blinked, looking at me as if through new eyes. "How wealthy is wealthy?"

I shrugged.

"No, really. Are we talking wealthy enough to own Thor's Shipbuilding or wealthy enough to own your own country?"

I hesitated, wincing. "Aye, the latter."

She fell back in her chair, the pies forgotten. "Ian... are you saying you're the heir to a fortune?"

"Aye, and if it weren't for the fact I'm the only child of my Mam, I'd have long since bowed out of ever taking even a cent of the cursed lot."

"Your mother?"

I blew out a breath. "She's got her own money. And a lot of it. If she were to die before my father, and I've left the family...."

"It'd all go to your father. I understand." Liv nodded.

"Do ye? Cause I don't. It's petty, and I hate that I'm this kind of man."

"Ian." She reached across the table, linking

our fingers. "It's okay. The man hurt you. Worse, he hurt someone you love. I do believe you're allowed to be petty sometimes."

I tried to summon a smile but suspected it looked more like a grimace. "I've not spoken to the man in over fifteen years, Liv. Not since leaving home."

"But you go back?"

"Aye. See my siblings and Mum. Nan's passed now, but Mum's still lively. Has her sisters and such over there. Tried to convince her to come here, but she says there's nothing for her." I glanced at Liv's stomach. "I'll admit to not being above using our wee bairn to tempt her."

Liv smiled, and I was struck once again by her beauty. "Bribe away. Who knows, maybe you'll be successful this time." She tilted her head to one side. "Did you know your accent gets stronger when you talk about home?"

I shook my head.

"It does. It's... lovely. I hope our baby picks up a little of it."

"But not the red hair?" I asked, glad for the distraction.

She grinned, eyeing my beard. "Oh, I don't know. I think it's starting to grow on me."

I lifted her hand, pressing a kiss to her palm, watching as her big blue eyes grew round, focusing on where my lips met her soft skin.

"Thank ye, Liv. For listening and understanding. And for... well, carrying my baby and letting me be a part of this."

Her face softened, and I caught a glimpse of ... something. Something naked and raw that had the power to devastate me.

"Right. Well." She shook me off, the look gone as quickly as it had appeared.

She settled back in her seat and reached for her fork once more. "That's done. Let me eat pie, and then we'll call them from the car. Nice and brief. Keep it short. We'll go from there, shall we?"

"Could we...." I swallowed. "Could you give me more time?"

Liv watched me, her head tilting to one side. It was so like her brother's that I nearly smiled.

"Alright." She stabbed her fork into her pie. "You tell me when you're ready, okay?"

I nodded, watching her begin to devour the pastries with a single-mindedness I couldn't help but admire.

As she ate, my mind replayed that look, and I couldn't help but wonder, did Liv want more with me?

CHAPTER 11

"Ian? I'm home!" I called, stamping my feet at the door to his mud room.

"Down the hall," he called back, his voice carrying.

"Fine, I'll get the groceries," I muttered, kicking off my boots. With a grunt, I hauled the bags up, carrying them into the house. I dumped them in the kitchen, tossing the cold stuff in the fridge before heading off in search of Ian.

His house wasn't big for a man who could, apparently, afford castles. Just four bedrooms and two baths. A family home for a man who, until recently, hadn't even had a girlfriend.

Well, now he's got a live-in baby momma and rapidly approaching child.

I found him in the third bedroom, paintbrush in hand.

"What do ye think?" he asked, gesturing at the wall.

"Oh, Ian."

My hands flew to my lips, my heart practically exploding as I took in the mural.

"Now, don't be getting all sentimental," he warned, waggling the paintbrush in my direction. "Twasn't all me. Your brother came over and helped. Rune's the one that came up with the idea, even drew all the lines. I just have to not fuck it up when painting."

The mural stretched along the wall where I'd planned to place the crib, a sky scene, hot air balloons filled with cute little animals bobbed merrily amongst the clouds.

"It's perfect," I whispered. "Absolutely perfect."

He turned, looping an arm over my shoulder and surveying his work. "Not bad. Needs a few coats, but she's coming along."

My body react to his touch in what was fast becoming predictable.

Forgive me, Father, for I am about to sin. Again. Only this time, I can't get pregnant.

I twisted, giving in to desire, tired of

spending my nights alone and my days struggling against my growing need for Ian.

We'd been living together for just over a week, and I'd never been hotter. My dreams the last few nights had centred entirely on that fucking boathouse and Ian fisting his cock. We'd explored positions I wasn't even sure existed outside of my dreams, and each day I'd woken hotter, wetter and more wrung out than the last.

Incoming!

I fisted his hair, yanking his head down until I could smash my lips to his.

He let out a startled yelp, the paintbrush crashing to the ground as we both tripped backwards, stumbling as I threw him off balance.

"Liv, what are ye—"

"Speak now and say no, or fuck me. God, Ian. You're driving me crazy."

His mouth crashed down on mine, his tongue delving as he feasted. I felt his cock grow thick and rigid against my belly.

Yes!

"What took you so long?" He asked, his fingers unsnapping each of the buttons of my coat.

"God knows," I answered with a laugh, nipping at his bottom lip. "But doesn't it feel good now?"

"Like I'm burning," he admitted, tossing off my coat, his hands dropping to the bottom of my sweater. "Ye're a saucy wench, my Liv. Now shut your mouth and let me concentrate."

I tipped my head back, my eyelids drifting shut as he stripped me, his hot mouth pausing to taste each inch of revealed skin.

"Aye, I remember these," he whispered, his voice rough and heavy as he cupped my breasts, gently stroking thumbs over my erect nipples.

I whimpered, shocked at their sensitivity.

"Mm, let me take care of you." He bent, laving one breast then the other, back and forth until my body screamed for release, a tight, wet heat boiling deep within me.

"Ian!"

"I think I told ye to hush," he said, pulling back. "Now you want me to continue or…?"

I glared at him, wanting desperately to move back. Finding myself instead pushing forward, rocking my body against his, needy and searching for release.

"Good lass." His praise set something off in me, a bone-deep ache tightening all the muscles in me.

I throbbed with need. My body nothing more than an extension of pleasure.

Touch me. Touch me. Touch me.

I silently pleaded, begged, bargained as Ian stepped back, leisurely stripping his paint-spattered clothing from his body.

Oh, my.

In the light of day, he looked different to the night of the wedding. His body was bigger, harder, heftier. Ian had no six-pack, he was what they'd call fat strong, his body all thickness and bulk. I loved it.

With no alcohol in my system to blur my vision or memory, I took him in, watching as he stepped out of his pants, leaving him in the skin in which he was born.

Perfection.

He reached for my jeans, stripping me of pants and underwear. He dropped to his knees, helping me step free, then reached for my socks, pausing when I stilled him with a shake of my head.

"Sorry, not sexy, but my feet are ice."

He chuckled, cupping one ankle and pressing a kiss to the inside of my thigh. "Everything you do is sexy, Liv. You should know that by now. From the first time I saw ye to this moment right now, you've always been the most beautiful woman in the room."

Pleasure bloomed in me, curling out and filling all the little corners of my soul.

"Add to your looks your personality, your love, your spark– it's too much for a man to resist." He pressed a kiss to my inner thigh, his tongue gliding along the sensitive skin. "I've a mighty craving for ye, lass. Now let me taste."

He licked his way up my thighs, pausing as he came to their apex, his hot breath a tease as I waited in desperate anticipation.

Finally, he leaned in, his lips and tongue a welcome balm to my over-sensitive skin.

"Yes!" I cried, my head falling back, hands gripping his shoulders. "Ian!"

He made soothing noises as he devoured me, his tongue an unrelenting pleasure.

My body coiled, my thighs quivering as he played with me, stoking me, his tongue laving my sensitive flesh before dancing away, only to build me back again.

Now, now, now, now, now!

As if hearing my silent plea, he changed tack, sucking roughly on my clit, ripping me straight into orgasm, the intensity overwhelming as I crashed head-first into pleasure.

He helped me down to the floor, gathering me in, and petting me as if I needed comfort. Perhaps I did, but I needed him more.

I reached between us, snaking a hand out

until I could grip his length, stroking him in a tight fist.

"Fuck!" He hissed, burying his head in my neck and nipping at the sensitive skin. "Ye filthy wench, harder."

Perhaps I should have been outraged with how he spoke to me, ordering me this way and that. But his tone, the gravel of need that threaded through his voice, it all worked together to drive me higher.

"Let me taste you."

He allowed it, guiding me down, holding his cock in one tight fist as I hovered my mouth for a moment before darting my tongue out to catch a salty drop of precum.

Yes.

His scent surrounded me, his unique mix of soap and sawdust, and the sharp bite of paint. I sucked him deep, my tongue dancing as I thrust forward and back, hollowing out my cheeks to fuck his cock with my mouth.

"Liv! Fuck!" Curses spilled from his mouth as he arched back, his head dropping, his body tight and focused.

Mine. All mine.

He allowed me to control him for but a few moments, my tongue and mouth overruling all of him. Then he hauled me up his body, positioning me just so and thrusting up and into me, filling me with his big cock, fucking me with wild, possessive need.

"Ian!"

"Take it, take me. All of me!" He barked, hands gripping my hips, holding me in place as his cock ravaged my tender flesh. "Gotta fuck you. Gotta make you see...."

I wanted to ask what I was meant to see, but the thought was swept away in a tidal wave of pleasure as my second orgasm crashed over me, shaking my body, ripping a hoarse scream from my throat.

Into me, Ian emptied himself, his body heaving, praises and curses by equal measures falling from his lips and my body milked his, both of us dropping to the floor in a clash of limbs and secret lies.

You can't love with only your body, Liv. He needs to know.

It's been him. It's always been him. It is him. He's your one, Liv. And you have to tell him.

God help me.

CHAPTER 12

Ian

I straightened my collar, staring at myself in the mirror.

Thanksgiving dinner with the Larsson's. I'd just finished a shift at work, pulling an extra day to get a project over a line for a particularly VIP client. I was meeting Liv at dinner and was running a little late.

It wouldn't be the first nor the last time I'd be invited to these events, but it was certainly the first one I'd attended where I was in love with their daughter. I wanted to make a good impression.

You need to tell her, ye daft goat.

It'd been over a week since Liv and I had come together. Within the space of a few hours she'd gone from roommate and mother of my child, to lover.

Hot as fuck lover.

Tell her!

We could barely keep our hands off each other, breaking in each room in the house, some multiple times over. I'd become addicted to her kisses, to her sweet little moans and harsh, needy screams. I craved the way she clutched me as she came, her body staking a claim on mine, branding me in a way I knew I'd never escape.

Tell her!

With a curse I turned away from the mirror, palming the mobile in my pocket.

There was only one thing preventing me from telling Liv I loved her, it was the same thing that plagued me each night as I fell asleep– what if I turned into my father?

We'd yet to call my mother with the good news, each time I'd put Liv off, making up some excuse about time zones or plans. In reality, I feared nothing more than my mother's affirmation that I'd be a terrible father.

With a deep breath I pulled the phone from my pocket, dialing the number. It rang three times before she picked up.

"Hello?"

"Mam, it's me, Ian."

My throat tightened as I heard her exclamation of surprise and delight.

"My prodigal son! I thought I'd never hear from you! What is happening over there in Astipia?"

"Mum, I have something to tell you. You remember Liv?"

"Aye, the Larsson girl. The elder one, I believe?"

"Aye." I swallowed, my stomach clenching. "She's pregnant. It's mine."

I heard her breath catch, a little hiccup of emotion.

"Oh, Ian." Her voice broke, a sob coming down the line.

My eyes screwed shut, despair overtaking me.

It's true then. I'm just like him.

"Congratulations, a wee bairn. Oh, my son, oh my dear, dear boy." She sobbed down the phone, but her tone and words broke through my cloud.

"Wait, congratulations?"

"Aye, congratulations! What? You expected me to curse you?"

"I..." I stumbled, needing to purge my greatest fear. "I worried you'd say I was like him."

Her breath caught; the phone line silent for a long moment.

"Oh, my darling.... I know you don't understand your father, or me for that matter. But no, Ian, ye're not like him. Ye never were, and never will be. You're a good man. You love with all your heart. And you'll treat that wee bairn better than anyone ever could."

She sighed. "Your father is a complicated man, and yes, I know what he is. But I love him. I know you'll never understand but that's okay, Ian. It truly is. Because I know you'll fight tooth and nail for your woman. You'll treat her like a queen and make her the centre of your world."

Her voice caught, and for a moment, I worried the line had dropped.

"I love you, son. So much. I'm so proud of you and what you've become. Never forget that."

"I love you too, Mam." I swallowed around the lump in my throat. "And perhaps, when the babe is born, you might like to come over for a visit?"

"Ooch, ye canna stop me!"

We spoke for a little while about life and Liv and love. I knew then I'd never understand my mother, but I had to let go of the fear and hate that had held me back from living my life. As we hung up, it struck me what a fool I'd been. For years I'd pushed Liv away, replacing my attraction with antagonism, all in an effort to avoid becoming the man I most feared.

This life, this love, this baby could have all been but a dream.

A sudden need to tell Liv drove me out of the bathroom, sending me running for my truck.

God, how could ye have been so stupid? Anyone could have swept her up.

Possession burned through me, raging until I couldn't tell passion from anger. I pulled up at the Larsson's, thundering up their walk to the front door. I threw it open with a crash, my gaze taking in the entry, ears strained for Liv's voice.

Her laughter came from the kitchen, and I headed in that direction at a fast clip, rounding the corner in time to see lift a forkful of pie to her lips.

"Liv Jemma Larsson!" I boomed, stopping to point at her. "You need to stop what you're doing and listen to me."

Everyone in the room fell silent. I vaguely registered that a young, good-looking, if vaguely familiar, man sat beside Astrid at the dinner table, but my focus was centred on Liv.

She considered me for a moment, her eyes flashing. Slowly, deliberately, she raised the fork to her lips, her gaze locked with mine, taking a bit of the pastry.

You saucy wench, I'm gonna spank you for that later.

I sucked in a breath. "Liv, I love you. I've loved ye since the moment I set eyes on you ten years ago. Ye were wearing a wee summer dress with a bikini underneath. We were picnicking on a boat, your brother thinking he'd been a right clever one by taking me out on the ocean to test my sea legs."

"Hey!" Erik cried, crossing his arms. "It was a good idea!"

We both ignored him.

"I thought I'd died and gone to heaven, seeing such a pretty girl on that boat. Then you gave me the bird and bomb-dived into the ocean, sending sass my way. Ever since we've been locked in a battle of wills, you and me. And I love it. I love how ye keep me on my toes. I love how you force me to be a better man. I love that you're pregnant with our baby, and that I've no doubt the wee one will be just as sassy and sweet as her gorgeous mother."

I crossed the room, hauling her into my arms, loving how she wrapped herself around me just as tight.

"You're gonna be an amazing mother, Liv. But I want more for you too. I'm gonna help you build your empire. I'm gonna be there, supporting you, giving you whatever you need to be the woman you want to be. To set the example for all our children that they get to dream and succeed. You're more than I've ever thought I could have. You're more than my heart, my Liv. You're my soul. I love you, and I want to marry ye. Tomorrow, if possible. But any day that works for you, I'll be there."

I kissed her, not waiting for an answer as around the room, her family watched.

I pulled back, Liv's eyelids fluttered open, her expression a little dazed.

"Liv?" her mother called. "Do you have something to add to this conversation?"

Liv's lips quirked as her gaze met mine, amusement dancing in their depths.

There's the sparkle I love.

"Ditto," she said with a laugh. "Only, you know, with you being a great dad."

The family collectively sighed, eyes rolling, heads shaking, but it was enough for me.

"You love me, lass?" I asked, cupping her cheek and brushing her complex braid out of my way.

"Yes," she said softly, a soft flush tinting her face. "I suspect I've loved you from the beginning as well. These last few years... Ian, you've been a constant for me. With your little judgmental smirk and knowing eye rolls."

I laughed, delighted with her sass.

She sobered, reaching out to capture one of my hands, placing it on the swell of her tiny baby bump. "I love you, Ian Campbell. This baby, how you've jumped in with both feet, the care you're showing me? All of it reads love. Maybe our way has been a little backward, but it's ours. And I love that. I love you."

My heart swelled, and I feared my large body would split in two attempting to contain my happiness and delight in this woman.

"This calls for—shit! What can pregnant women drink in celebration?" Astrid asked the group. "Like... sparkling grape juice? Apple juice? Hardly seems worth the effort."

"Apple juice," my mother declared. "Sune, run to the store and get some."

"I'm not bloody going to the shops to get juice. It's fucking thanksgiving. It's either going to bare, closed or busier than a mosquito on a nudist beach."

"Sune!"

"Someone should probably call Gunnar and Ella, right?" Erik asked, bouncing a giggling Leif on one knee. "Or maybe not? They're with the Bronzes, right? That family is mental. Truly mental."

"Wait, *you guys* think they're crazy?" Gabby asked. "What did they do?"

"Don't you remember the wedding?" Laura asked, shuffling around the kitchen. "Ella's brothers did that crazy spontaneous speech...."

I pressed my forehead against Liv's, loving the chatter and laughter around us.

"You sure you want to join this madhouse?" Liv asked softly.

"Lass, if ye haven't noticed, I already have."

She laughed, pressing a jubilant kiss to my mouth before rocking back. "Ring?"

"We'll get you one when you're not bloated."

"Good thinking. Wedding?"

"I'd marry ye at Thor's Shipbuilding in that tiny apartment while you're wearing a robe if ye so wish. Honest to God, Livvy, wherever, whenever, however, ye want you can have it."

She eyed me, a teasing gleam in her eye. "And you're *how* rich exactly?"

I laughed, wrapping an arm around her and pulling her in for another kiss.

EPILOGUE ONE

"You motherfucker!" I screamed, bearing down as the contraction tore me apart. "You fucking motherfucker!"

"Breathe, love. Come on, remember what the coach said? One, two, three. One, two—"

"I'm gonna smash you in the face if you don't get me some drugs this instance!"

"Too late," Dr. Kristen said cheerfully from her position at my nether regions. "This little bubba is on its way. Now get ready, the next contraction will be here right about...."

We'd been out on the boat. The motherfucking boat. The boat Ian had made for me as a wedding gift. This kid hadn't been due for another week and I'd like the idea of spending some alone time together.

An hour out, the contractions had started, no biggie. First baby, we had plenty of time.

Half an hour later I was screaming at Ian to turn this fucking boat around and get me to the hospital. He'd done so, and we'd been rushed straight through, the paramedics having told me I was nearly ready to start pushing.

No fucking way was I ready to start pushing.

No.

Fucking.

Way.

"Push!"

With a hoarse scream, I bore down, every single cell in my body clenching, pain turning everything into a haze of red and grey.

Dimly, I heard Ian's encouragement, and the doctor's and nurses' praise. But all my focus remained on getting this child of Satan from my body.

"One more!"

I pushed again, screaming as my baby finally slid from my body, entering the world.

"She's here!" Kristen crowed, checking her over. "And she's perfect momma. Well done!"

With practice she laid the now crying infant on my chest, Ian crowding in beside me.

My body clenched, pushing out the afterbirth, but I barely felt it, such was my joy as I took in my precious daughter's tiny face.

"Hello, darling." Ian cooed beside me. "Go on, Mummy, what's her name?"

"Brenna," I decided, staring at our perfect bundle. "It means sword."

"Perfect," Ian agreed, pressing a kiss to my temple. "As perfect as her fierce mother."

I looked up at him, our daughter in my arms, tears in my eyes, love in my heart.

"Any regrets?"

"Only one," he admitted as the nurses and Kristen cleaned me up.

"Really?"

"Mm." He leaned down; his lips close to mine. "Only that I waited so long before claiming you. We could have had this wee precious girl a long time ago."

I laughed, tears streaking down my face. "I don't know, this seems pretty perfect to me."

"It does indeed. I love you, Livvy."

I lifted my chin, kissing him, letting Ian feel my love.

EPILOGUE TWO

Ian

My phone vibrated in my pocket. I hit the kill switch, the table saw slowing to a stop as I stepped back, pulling off my ear muffs and answering the call.

"Liv?"

"Ian, the school called. Your daughter staged a protest at lunch. She's refusing to eat the cafeteria food until they improve the offerings. She managed to get half her class to do the same. We've got a meeting with the school at three."

I hid a laugh behind a cough. "Liv, she's in first grade."

"I know! You think I don't know that? Ian, what have we created?"

"We? Ooch, love, I told ye from day one, any girl child of ours was gonna be hellfire and brimstone with a Mam like you."

Liv made a sound somewhere between a laugh, a cry and a sigh. "Thank God, Oili isn't as much of a handful."

Our second daughter took after me, sweet as pie.

"Ah, but we both know Shelby is just waiting for her chance to shine."

Our youngest had just turned two and hit it with a vengeance. A tiny dictator, she'd wrapped the entire family around her fearsome little pinky. She'd either change the world or destroy it.

"Let's pray this next one is sweet."

My heart skipped. "Next one?"

Liv paused, her voice catching. "I mean... I'm not pregnant but with the production company going so well, and me delegating more... I just thought... maybe... if you wanted to...."

"Woman, get home. Now."

I began to strip off my safety gear, my body hardening at the idea of impregnating my wife. Again. Liv in full bloom was a glorious sight to behold.

"Wait, right now? I have a meeting with a crew about that—"

"Now!"

"Pushy." She didn't sound displeased. But she'd be getting a little spank for the protesting anyway.

"Love ye, Liv."

"Love you too, Sasquatch."

"You on your way?"

"I'll be there in ten. And you better bring that super sperm, I want to be pregnant by lunch tomorrow."

"I'll do my best."

"Mm, I can work with that."

———

Thank you so much for reading Ian and Liv! Their book took much longer to write than normal mostly because all Liv wanted to do was eat pie. Seriously, there are about five scenes that I deleted where it was just Liv eating pie.

Next up is The Christmas Contract, featuring Astrid and a certain good-looking Aussie.

Desperate for more Ian and Liv? Check out the bonus chapter at EvieMitchell.com

ABOUT THE AUTHOR

Hey, I'm Evie Mitchell.
I'm a thirty-something romance author (she/her/hers) living with disability. I believe in inclusion, accessibility, and fierce romance. My loves include steamy romance novels, my sexy husband, our THREE sausage dogs (THE FUR!!!), and my ever-growing collection of book-related mugs.

As a woman with a diverse work history, including in areas such as hospitality, retail, emergency response, event management, human rights, disability access, and security— my books are filled with true stories (bridezillas), worst-case scenarios (malfunctioning zippers), and my favorite tropes (one-bed).

I'm a strong proponent of #OwnVoices, and specialize in fiercely inclusive happily ever afters.

EvieMitchell.com
Socials: @EvieMitchellAuthor

ALSO BY EVIE MITCHELL

All Access Series

Knot My Type

Love Flushed

Darn Knit All

Larsson Siblings

Thunder Thighs

Clean Sweep

The X-List

The Christmas Contract

The A-List

Capricorn Cove

The Shake-up

Double the D

Muffin Top

The Mrs. Clause

New Year, Knew You

Double Breasted

As You Wish

You Sleigh Me

Meat Load

Resolution Revolution

Dogg Pack

Puppy Love

Bad English

The Frock Up

Pier Pressure

Trick or Trent

New Year's Faye

Reigning Hearts

The Marriage Claim

Silent Knight

Men of Trinity Bay

Kink in the Road

Nameless Souls MC

Runner

Wrath

Ghost

Shield

Elliot Security

Rough Edge
Bleeding Edge